PUFFIN BOOKS

JAZ SANTOS vs THE WORLD

About the Author

Priscilla Mante is a London-based writer from Glasgow. She spent several years delivering arts, literacy and cultural programmes to young people and currently works in corporate communications. *Jaz Santos vs. the World* is her debut novel.

JAZ SANTOS vs THE WORLD

Priscilla Mante

PUFFIN

PUFFIN BOOKS

UK | USA | Canada | Ireland | Australia
India | New Zealand | South Africa

Puffin Books is part of the Penguin Random House group of companies
whose addresses can be found at global.penguinrandomhouse.com.

www.penguin.co.uk
www.puffin.co.uk
www.ladybird.co.uk

Penguin
Random House
UK

First published 2021
002

Text copyright © Priscilla Mante, 2021
Interior illustrations by Jan Bielecki and Sophia Watts
Interior illustrations copyright © Penguin Books Ltd, 2021

The moral right of the author and illustrators has been asserted

The recipe included at the end of this book may not be suitable for those
with food allergies or intolerances. Please check the recipe carefully for the
presence of any ingredients or substances that may cause an adverse reaction
if consumed by those with any food allergy or intolerance. This recipe has not been
formally tested and the publisher accepts no responsibility or liability for it.

Set in 13/18.5 pt Sabon LT Std
Typeset by Jouve (UK), Milton Keynes
Printed and bound in Great Britain by Clays Ltd, Elcograf S.p.A.

The authorized representative in the EEA is Penguin Random House Ireland,
Morrison Chambers, 32 Nassau Street, Dublin DO2 YH68

A CIP catalogue record for this book is available from the British Library

ISBN: 978-0-241-48200-1

All correspondence to:
Puffin Books, Penguin Random House Children's
One Embassy Gardens, 8 Viaduct Gardens, London SW11 7BW

To everyone who finds the courage to dream

Prologue

Olá! You've probably heard of me and the Bramrock Stars before. If you haven't, you will have soon because we're almost famous. Well, first things first: let me introduce myself since you'll be hearing a lot from me. I'm left striker for the Stars. I'm in Year 6 at Bramrock Primary School in a town called Bramrock, which is a half-hour drive from Brighton. Oops – I've forgotten to tell you my name! Well, to make it worth the wait, I'll do it in Portuguese, shall I? *Meu nome é Jasmina Santos-Campbell.* That means, 'My name is Jasmina Santos-Campbell.' Don't bother about remembering all of that, though – nearly everyone calls me Jaz! That is, unless I'm in trouble, which as you'll find out happens quite a lot . . . but more about that later. Quite honestly, I'm not sure where to start, but Dad always says the beginning is a good place, so that's where I'll go. Right back to the beginning . . .

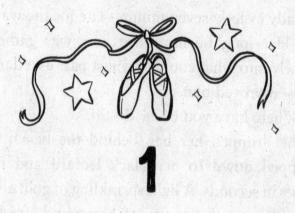

1

Dizzy Dancers

Every corner of Bramrock Primary dance studio was buzzing with excited dancers. It was the last class before we got into full rehearsal mode for the annual showcase. This year Ms Morgan's dance club were putting on a jazz-ballet version of *Alice in Wonderland* called *Spinning Alices*. We were going to perform the story of *Alice in Wonderland* through a series of specially choreographed dances.

I scanned the busy dance hall, searching for Charligh. The door swung open and in burst my best friend, looking so relaxed, as if we weren't already exactly seven minutes late for the warm-up. Her long burnt-orange hair was gathered loosely into what could only just pass as a dance-class-approved bun.

'Where have you been?' I said.

She dropped her bag behind the bench and stripped down to her black leotard and pink tights in seconds. A light sprinkling of gold glitter twinkled on the apples of her round, freckled cheeks.

'How about the stage diva sprinkles her glitter dust *after* dance class next time?' I said as we hurried over to join the others at the barre.

Charligh raised her left eyebrow in a perfect arch. 'Since when did Her Royal Lateness care about being on time for anything? You've made us late –' Charligh wiggled her fingers, pretending to tally it up – '*four hundred and forty-four* times this year alone.' Charligh's middle name was Drama. Well, not really, but it should have been. She exaggerated everything, although she was just about right in her calculation of my lateness record.

'Come on, girls! Last ones to get started again?' Ms Morgan swept through the hall, observing everyone's form and ensuring our outfits were just as she wanted.

We took up our positions at the barre. After all, we didn't want to be told more than once by Ms Morgan. She had a special saying about repeating instructions. It was 'twice, not so nice'.

I started my warm-up with a simple mix of pliés and demi-pliés. I looked at Charligh. 'This is our last chance to impress Ms Morgan before she decides on who is playing what in *Spinning Alices*,' I said.

'Either of you'll be lucky to even get in the chorus line,' Rosie Calderwood observed, butting in. 'Everyone knows I'm the best dancer and I'll get the lead role.' She flashed a dimpled smile that didn't reach her ice-blue eyes and smoothed her chocolate-brown hair that was already tucked neatly into a perfect bun.

Now, Ridiculous Rosie is *definitely* not part of my team. In fact, she's kind of a bad guy in this story, so any time she shows up you might want to boo, really loud. Rosie's the leader of the VIPs and, in case you can't tell, she is basically my arch-nemesis.

'Everyone knows Rosie will get the leading role,' Erica Waters gushed like a drippy tap. So Erica is pretty much Rosie's echo. She wasn't too bad until last year, when she was recruited into the VIPs along with Rosie's other sidekick, Summer Singh. Charligh and I call them the Very Irritating People. They had never actually told us what VIP stood for, so we could only assume, based on the evidence . . . I mean, the entire class knew exactly how many times Rosie had been to Orlando, Florida (three times), and just how much spending money she got for her family's annual shopping weekend to Paris (a thousand euros) and how big their villa in Spain was (very big).

Charligh tottered on one leg, stretching the other as high as she could. 'Rosie, do you take extra lessons on the side to become so good – or does it just come naturally to you?'

'Good at what?' Rosie said with her trademark smugness.

'Being incredibly annoying, of course,' Charligh replied.

I snorted.

'You cheeky little –' Rosie hissed.

She was cut short by Ms Morgan's three loud claps – her signal that warm-up was over. We gathered together on the mats in front of her.

'As you all know, this is our last rehearsal before Saturday, when we'll begin on all the group and solo routines for *Spinning Alices*.' She looked round at everyone. 'Consider this a final audition, because I still haven't made my decision on the lead solos. I have an idea, of course, but it's not too late to dazzle me today.'

I grinned at Charligh. I knew it! There was still time to show Ms Morgan that I could be lead soloist at this year's showcase. Mãe (you pronounce it like 'my', by the way, and it's Portuguese for 'mum') bought four tickets last year – one each for her, Dad and my brother Jordan, and the fourth for her youngest sister, my Aunty Bella. Mãe hadn't even made it to any of my parents' evenings for the last two years – Dad was so used to attending by himself now. But there she was at last year's showcase in the front row. It made me feel all sparkly inside when I took the final bow with everyone and heard her cheers above the crowd.

'OK, dancers! Split up into your groups of four. It's time for the mirror routine,' Ms Morgan said.

For the mirror routine, each person in the group took a different corner of the room and then performed an identical set of steps so that all four met in the middle. I was in a group with the K triplets from Year 5, so I sat down next to Katy, Keeley and Karina to wait our turn.

This year the showcase was going to be even more special. An army of butterflies took off in my stomach. My mother, who was the best dressmaker in all of Bramrock, was going to make the costumes. Imagine how proud she would be if I turned out to be the girl she had to measure for the grand solo dance at the end? I sat up, back straight, crossing my legs neatly, and noticed a plum-coloured bruise on my ankle. It must have been the vicious tackle Zach Bacon went in for today at lunchtime. *The next time I play him at football*, I thought, *I'll run rings round him*. I'd win the tackle, dribble fast and tight, flick the ball up and head it into the goal. Catching a look at my reflection in the mirrored wall, I realized I looked a bit silly because I'd been miming the actions. I quickly held my head and legs still before anyone saw. Too late.

Rosie waltzed over. 'You're such a weird loser, Jaz. What are you doing – throwing your head about like that? You're an awkward duckling who'll never grow into a graceful swan,' she sneered.

I'd been attending Ms Morgan's after-school dance club twice a week for two years now, learning ballet, jazz and modern dance, but I knew I could be a bit of an elephant among the more dainty dancers. I did goof around sometimes, but even when I tried my hardest, my grands jetés or straddle jumps never seemed to feel as easy to me as dribbling a football down the wing. Still, I wasn't going to let Ridiculous Rosie have the last word.

'Maybe the next time you go on one of your *amazing* holidays, your family can do us all a favour and just leave you there?'

Ms Morgan looked over. 'Jaz! I need you to stop distracting Rosie. We've all worked very hard to get our standards up this term. I won't let you spoil it for everyone.'

The rest of my group were standing in their positions, ready to do the drill. I folded my arms, stung by Ms Morgan's comments. It was dreadfully unfair of her not to notice that Rosie had started it – but then teachers never, ever noticed when Rosie did that sort of thing. Perhaps there was an invisible halo above her smug, heart-shaped face that made everyone treat her like an angel. As I twirled across the studio, I stared hard in the mirror to make sure there weren't invisible horns above my head, because I always got blamed for everything.

This year it *had* to be different. Mãe and Dad had been arguing a lot lately. And even when they weren't actually snapping at each other, there was this horrid feeling in the air that made me feel they were going to start. I had to stop getting into trouble so much because it was just one more thing for them to fight about – like the way they argued over the comments on my report card in Year 5, which were mostly 'must try harder', 'needs to pay more attention' and 'can be a bit disruptive'. So seeing me standing on the stage with a lead part in *Spinning Alices* wouldn't fix everything, but it would help. I could just picture it now: a star-shaped spotlight shining on me, Mãe and Dad crying tears of pride – and Rosie scowling from the shadows . . .

'Ouf!' gasped Katy. She'd collided with me as I began my second pirouette, crashing me out of my dream.

Ms Morgan paused the music. 'OK, let's try that again with the last group. Some of us –' she looked pointedly at me – 'are not paying attention. We need to get this right. How we make our entrance sets the tone for the entire performance. The plan is to make a dramatic entrance, not a comedic one.'

I ignored the snickers of Rosie and Erica from behind me and took a deep breath. *Focus*, I told myself. *Grand jeté. Plié. One, two, three. Pirouette, pirouette, pirou–*

BANG!

This time I skidded all the way past Katy and my elbow connected with the mirrored wall. Then it happened. It always appeared at the worst time. The Laugh was creeping up on me like a rising tidal wave. I tried to keep it down but the pressure was unbearable. It surged in my belly, pulsed up my chest and throat, and chugged out through my mouth and nose.

'Sorry, I'll just –' I spluttered.

Ms Morgan didn't let me finish. 'Take five minutes, Jaz. You can just sit over there and come back when you're ready to stop being silly,' she said. My cheeks burned as I saw a pleased smile flicker across Rosie's face now that I'd given her the chance to steal the spotlight. I watched her land gracefully on her feet after a series of three perfect pirouettes.

It was boring watching the others practise, so I decided to pretend I was actually on the bench, ready to run out on to the pitch to play for England in the finals of the next Women's World Cup. A sports commentator was announcing my arrival on the field . . .

Newly signed Jaz Santos-Campbell runs on to the pitch and immediately gets possession of the ball. She speeds down the centre . . . through three Italian defenders, passes neatly to Rachel Yankey on the wing, who takes it wide before sending it back in a perfect cross to Jaz . . . who SLAMS it in the back of the net with that great left foot in the final minute of play! What a pair of champions! Their supporters have hope again . . . it looks like they could win this . . . Wembley has never seen such an incredible final . . .!

The fans were chanting . . . *Jaz! Jaz! She's our star! Jaz! Jaz! . . .*

'Jaz! *Jasmina!*' Ms Morgan said loudly. I leaped to my feet, hoping she hadn't been shouting my name for too long. 'If you'd like to join us from whichever world you've drifted off to, you're more than welcome.'

Luckily we'd moved on from those pesky pirouettes and it was time to practise a new dance. It was a mix of jazz and ballet. Ms Morgan came over to my group, just as it was my turn. I took a deep breath, listening to the music as I moved to the upbeat jazz rhythm, and ended in an arabesque: front leg steady, back leg stretched out, and head tilted upwards. The best way for me to stay perfectly still was to imagine I had my size-five football balancing on my head. I held my breath while Ms Morgan's eyes focused on me.

'Excellent,' she said briskly, before she moved on. I exhaled and relaxed from my position. A seal of approval from Ms Morgan. Finally!

Later, as Charligh and I filed out at the end of class, Ms Morgan stopped me. 'Can I have a word, Jaz?'

'Text me tonight,' Charligh said in a stage whisper. I gave her a small nod as the others zipped out past me.

Perhaps Ms Morgan was feeling bad about how terribly unfair she had been to me earlier. Maybe she was going to apologize because she had finally realized – and not a minute too soon – that it was me, and not Rosie, who had the potential to be a star dancer. My toes tingled. I was already expecting Ms Morgan to give me the biggest hint that she was going to choose *me* as the lead dancer. I giggled, thinking of Rosie's face when I told her . . .

Ms Morgan sighed heavily. 'Jaz, do you still think this is funny?'

I frowned. Judging from the look on her face, maybe I'd got the wrong end of the stick after all and that lead role wasn't quite mine . . . yet.

'You know what I'm going to say, don't you?' she continued, sounding even more impatient.

No, I didn't. I had absolutely no idea. That was part of the problem: I could never tell what the grown-ups were thinking. Take Fussy Forrest, for example, the deputy head-dragon – I mean deputy head*teacher* –

'Jaz! Are you even listening to me?' Ms Morgan said. 'You have the potential to be a good dancer, but you have to knuckle down. Do you think Rosie achieved the level she is at by picking fights and being disruptive?'

'But Rosie –' I protested

Ms Morgan held up her hand. 'I don't want to hear anything more about Rosie, or Erica or anyone else. You always have an excuse. My mind is made up. You're on report for the next week. I'll be watching you extra closely in dance and checking with all of your teachers to make sure you're behaving, paying attention and not bickering with Rosie.'

Her words rained down on me, her warning looming over me like a steely cloud. One week of ignoring all of Rosie's nasty digs. One week of concentrating during Fussy Forrest's boring classes. One. Whole. Week.

'Understood?' said Ms Morgan.

My stomach lurched, but I nodded. It was only one week, I told myself. I could do this . . . couldn't I?

2

Happy Families

I arrived at my house damp from the shower of rain and breathless after my ten-minute uphill cycle. Mãe had forgotten to drive over to pick me up. Again. Now I don't want you to think I'm complaining about my mum, because I'm not. If there was a Coolest Mum Ever award, it would definitely go to her. She speaks Portuguese *and* English, she doesn't nag me about homework, and she wears beautiful patterned headwraps that she makes from her own fabric. It was just that lately she'd been so busy. I'd have thought she'd have been pleased that everyone could see how talented she was at designing and making clothes. But instead she was so stressed, and was spending nearly all the time she used to spend with me and Jordan on getting through her orders for customers.

I dropped my bag in the hall and poked my head round the door to the back room, where Mãe worked on her designs. Her room reminded me of a sunny rainforest. The back wall was crowded with lanky ferns in terracotta pots. The plants leaned over, casting interesting shadows along the pale-yellow walls.

Mãe was sitting hunched over her sketchbook at the huge mahogany desk Dad had made for her. Her sewing machine was by her side. She gave a tiny cry and put her hand momentarily to her forehead. 'Ah, *minha anjinha*, my angel! I'm sorry. I forgot to pick you up again, didn't I? How was the *dança*?' In her left hand she held a charcoal pencil poised in mid-air.

'Hmm – OK,' I said, hoping she wouldn't ask any more questions. The last thing I wanted to tell her was that I was one step away from *not* getting to star in the showcase.

Mãe's tight dark curls were scrunched up on the top of her head, held by a turquoise silk scarf that made her hair stand up like a black crown. 'Are you hungry? Do you want me to cook something?' she asked. Already her pencil was back down on the paper, skating and flirting across it as she crafted one of her wonderful creations. The closest thing my mum got to cooking was bunging things in the microwave. What was the point of sweating over a hot stove when she could buy perfectly good ready meals from frozen-food stores? Or at least that's what she used to say before Dad took over all the cooking. Unlike Mãe, Dad loved sweating over hot stoves. He was good at cooking all kinds of healthy but tasty things. My favourite was his delicious homemade pizza.

'No, I'm not hungry, thanks, Mãe,' I said, hoping she couldn't hear the rumbling of my stomach. I didn't mind the ready meals too much, but the last thing I wanted was for Dad to come back and start arguing with her for feeding us 'junk food' again.

'OK, love. Your dad's running a bit late. He had an emergency call-out in Brighton.' My dad was a carpenter and worked for the council. He often got called out to fix things. 'So he'll pick Jordan up from orchestra practice on his way back,' Mãe said. She started chewing on her lip and her knuckles tightened over the pencil as she focused intently on what she was drawing. Mãe already seemed to have forgotten I was there, so I backed out of the room, leaving her to float off into her world of designs again.

In the kitchen, there was a pile of plates stacked up from breakfast and crumbs all over the green marble worktop. The magnolia vinyl floor was smeared with muddy grass stains near the back door where Mãe popped out to smoke. I hated her horrid cigarettes. So did Dad.

First, I packed what I could into the dishwasher until it was full, then I grabbed the long yellow rubber gloves hanging over the tap, thrust them on and hand-washed the rest. Next, I squirted Mr Strong lemon cleaner along the worktop and cooker. I scrubbed and wiped until the stove top gleamed and the worktop was rid of all the crumbs and spills. Last of all, I mopped the mucky floor. My arms were aching by the time I'd finished, but it was worth it to have the kitchen looking clean. *That's one less thing for them to fight over*, I thought as I went up to my room.

Tuesday night was mac and cheese night in our house. Dad always made it with a creamy, mouth-watering vegan 'cheese' sauce that wasn't actually made of cheese. Instead, he used a mix of coconut milk, cashew nuts and turmeric.

'Hey! Leave some for me,' I said. I was the last to sit down at the dinner table. Jordan was helping himself to the crusty browned part, the best bit, of the macaroni cheese. He was super annoying sometimes, but according to Charligh (and she reckons she should know because she has two) he was OK as far as brothers went.

'Plenty for everyone, *princesa*,' said Mãe.

'Yeah, plenty!' Jordan grinned. He was shovelling what seemed like half the dish on to his plate.

I gave him a swift kick under the table.

'Ow!' he said, letting go of the serving spoon.

I picked it up before it even hit the bowl again and served myself a generous portion. 'Right, plenty,' I said sweetly as I handed him back the spoon.

'So how was everyone's day?' Dad asked. He loved hearing about how Jordan and I had got on.

'Mr Bianci liked my interpretation of Mozart's *Sinfonia Concertante*. He thinks I have a good chance of making it into the National Youth Orchestra next year,' said Jordan. My brother played viola and piano, and was one of the youngest in Brighton Youth Orchestra.

'Wonderful!' said Mãe. 'I don't know where you get your musical talent because you certainly didn't get it from either of us.'

'Speak for yourself,' Dad said. 'Don't you remember how everyone would beg me to get up and sing whenever we had our karaoke nights?'

'How could I forget, Drew? Whenever we felt like some comedy, your singing was just the thing.'

I smiled. It was good to see my mum and dad joking around with each other again. Things had been so weird lately. If they weren't snapping at each other, they mostly weren't speaking at all. Maybe, just maybe, things were getting back to normal now – finally.

'And how did Favourite Daughter get on today at dance?' Dad said.

'I'm your only daughter, Dad.'

'OK. How did my Only Favourite Daughter do?'

I paused. My parents were getting on so well tonight I didn't want to be the one to ruin things. 'Ms Morgan reckons I have the potential to be one of the best dancers,' I said.

It wasn't a lie, right? Not really. I just wasn't telling the *whole* truth.

'You didn't tell me this earlier,' Mãe said. A smile danced across her face. 'It looks like I'll have to make the lead dancer's costume extra special now.'

I nodded vigorously. 'Ms Morgan said she didn't know what she would do without me . . . The class just wouldn't be the same.' I did feel a bit guilty, but then if I told them what had really happened, the mood would have curdled faster than that milk I left out of the fridge by mistake last week.

'She'd be daft not to choose you for the lead anyway,' said Dad firmly, even though he didn't know a thing about ballet and jazz.

Telling the whole truth about what teachers said never did any good.

After dinner, I took my ball out into the garden. The sky was the colour of baked apricots and a warm breeze blew through my curls, ruffling my fringe. Back when Dad used to play for the local team, Bramrock Rangers, in the Sunday league, we'd take turns practising shooting at goal. The 'goal' was two broad oak trees at the back of the garden that Dad had tied a bit of string between to form a crossbar. But everything changed after Dad injured his Achilles' tendon last year when taking a penalty kick. He'd been on crutches for months. Even though his injury was healed, he said he was taking a break from the Rangers, and he'd stopped practising with me too.

I couldn't wait to get out and kick a ball around. Football made everything better. The excitement when my feet made contact with the ball to dribble or kick, the spark that shot through me as I ran down the wings, and the pride when the ball rolled past the posts. In school, at dance and even at home . . . basically everywhere . . . I was always messing up. On the pitch, though, I understood the rules; I knew just how to dribble, and block and strike!

I'd been practising my keepy-uppies every night that week. Using my feet, knees or chest, I fought to keep the ball from touching the ground. My record was thirty-three and I was proud of it. The previous week Zach Bacon (whose record was thirty-one) sneered at me and said I played like a girl. I didn't mind playing like a girl – some of the best football players in the world were girls, like Saki Kumagai, Marta Vieira da Silva, Fran Kirby and of course my very favourite, Rachel Yankey. I chucked the ball on to the top of my left foot and began counting as I kicked it upwards . . . *One . . . two . . . three . . . four . . .* I dropped it after twenty-eight. I knew it didn't make sense, but a little niggling voice in my head said if I could beat my record it would be good luck and the arguments inside would stop for good. I tried again and got to thirty-one. *Not good enough*, I thought as I headed back in with the ball tucked under my arm.

The telly hummed softly downstairs. I could hear snippets from the ten o'clock news. Maybe my parents were sick of arguing now. I relaxed a little, thinking of the nice dinner we'd just had as I snuggled down in bed. I was still a bit worried about what Ms Morgan had said, but I was determined not to fail.

The TV kept getting a little bit louder every few minutes. I squirmed, willing myself to fall asleep so I wouldn't hear what was coming next. They always put the volume up when they were arguing.

Before long, bubbles of harsh words from yet another argument floated upstairs: *It's always about you, isn't it? . . . Drew, I can't speak to you like this . . . You keep avoiding . . . When are you going to discuss this like a reasonable adult?*

I could only hear bits of what they were saying, so I got out of bed and went down the stairs two at a time, trying to miss out the creaky steps. *Two, four, six, eight . . . OUCH!* I crashed down on my bottom and slid across the wooden floor in the hall. My right knee connected with the tall cornflower-blue vase. It wobbled nervously and I scrambled up to stop it rocking over.

'Is that you, princess? Is everything OK?' Dad called from the living room. He stuck his head round the door before I could even answer. He looked worried. 'You should be in bed, Jaz. It's really late. Is the TV disturbing you?' he asked.

'Yes, and I, erm . . . I wanted a drink of water.'

The words stuck in my mouth. I didn't have the heart to tell Dad that it was their angry words keeping me awake. He would feel so bad and that would give him and Mãe something else to argue about.

'Sorry, love.' He went into the kitchen and came out with a glass of water for me. 'We'll switch the TV off and go to bed too.' I thought that was a good idea; the skin around Dad's green eyes were dry and puffy. He didn't look as if he'd slept well for a while.

By the time I got back to bed, the TV was turned off, just like Dad said, and the house was totally quiet except for the occasional gurgle from the pipes. I heard one set of footsteps come up to my parents' room. I listened hard for the other, but it never came.

I gazed up at the luminous purple stars on my white ceiling and wished hard that I could be like one of them. I wished I could brighten the thickening darkness that was swallowing up my family.

3

Bake-off

Charligh and I weaved our way through the grey-topped tables to the back of the hall. We always sat at the broken half-table that had six seats instead of twelve. Naomie Osei and Steph Richardson made their way over to us, carrying strange-smelling hot dishes on their red plastic trays. Naomie and Steph are my other two best friends, although Charligh is my BBF (that's bestest best friend, if you didn't know).

I bit into my tuna-salad baguette, thankful once again that Dad made my lunch every day because, unlike Steph and Naomie, I didn't like school dinners. Out of nowhere, a gummy bear whizzed through the air. The orange sweet collided with the centre of Naomie's smooth dark-brown forehead. The other three of us turned, scanning the lunch hall for the culprit, but Naomie just rolled her eyes.

'They're so obvious,' she said wearily. Naomie dug her fork into something pale and wobbly, which the dinner ladies claimed was 'Chicken Surprise'.

Zach and his friends sniggered and stared at us from across the hall. If it wasn't for football, I don't think I would speak to any of the Year 6 boys. Ever. Unfortunately for me, most of the girls in my class didn't like football at all. So the Fabulous Four – that's me, Charligh, Naomie and Steph – had a theory to explain their behaviour. The year we were born, there was a science experiment conducted on all the baby boys, where part of their brain was removed. The part that made you not act like an annoying human being. It was the only logical explanation, right?

Half of the (half-brained) boys in our class had a crush on Naomie. OK, maybe not half . . .

more like *all* the boys. She'd won the Excellence in Science award for the school last year, and with her high cheekbones, glowing skin and big dark eyes she looked as if she could be a model. Naomie didn't want to be a model, though. She wanted to be an astrophysicist. I wasn't sure exactly what that was, but I knew that if anyone could do it, Naomie could. So, yeah, basically the Year 6 boys acted goofy to catch the attention of the smartest girl in the class. I know . . . like I said, science experiment?

'It's depressing how childish the boys in Year Six are,' Charligh groaned.

'They're even worse than they were in Year Five. Do you think they are ageing backwards?' Steph said, narrowing her pale-green eyes. Steph was school captain this term and she was about the most mature person in our class. She was one of Bramrock Primary's Eco-Champions. That meant she spent a lot of time creating posters and giving class presentations about climate change, how we could be kinder to the earth and all the creatures in it by doing things like recycling, turning off lights when we weren't using them and eating less meat.

'Olly seems OK. He picked me first for his team last time,' I said. Olly Fitzpatrick had only joined our class at the start of term a few weeks ago, but he had already put Zach's nose out of joint because he had taken his place as fastest runner in Year 6. Anyone who took Zach down a peg or two was OK in my book.

'Hmm, I suppose he may have missed out on the experiment,' said Naomie.

The hall had suddenly grown quiet. I looked round and saw that Olly, Zach and all that lot had vanished. As much as I hoped they'd been transported to a secret planet (where they'd be given new personalities before they came back to earth), I knew just where they had gone.

I stood up. 'I'd better head off to the football pitch. Zach would love it if I miss this game . . .'

'Which is exactly why you need to be there,' finished Charligh.

'Exactly!' I said, giving her a high five.

I played football with the boys most lunchtimes, and had done since the beginning of Year 5 – before that, I'd only practised with Dad in the garden and the park. The problem was, some of them didn't like a girl getting the ball off them, so they'd go in extra hard for tackles, or some wouldn't even pass to me. That just made me more determined to show them what I could do! I dribbled down the right wing with Zach and Sebastian coming at me from either side. I weaved round both of them, so they almost ran into each other, and then kicked the ball to Olly, who was standing in the centre. I ran behind him and he back-heeled the ball, then stepped out of the way, and – with a short, sharp kick – I tucked it into the back of the net with my left foot.

'Nice one, Jaz,' said Olly. He gave me a high five as the bell rang, signalling the end of lunch. My last-minute goal meant we won two–nil against Zach's side.

'You let a girl score,' I heard Zach taunt Theo Masanga, who was in goal.

'Yeah, the same girl who got the ball round you and Sebastian,' I shot back. His face went bright red as his friends snickered at him. I gave him my best smile as I jogged off the pitch to line up with the rest of the class.

*

I perched on a stool next to Charligh in the cookery room. I felt great. I'd scored the winning goal *and* now it was time for our weekly cooking class.

Mrs Tavella, the cookery teacher, was pretty cool in a grandma type of way. She always wore a wipe-clean floral apron and sensible flat shoes and she had wispy silvery hair always tucked neatly behind her ears. In Year 6 at Bramrock Primary, to help us prepare for secondary school, we had different teachers for some lessons, like music and cooking, and sometimes we had PSHE (personal, social, health and economic education) taught by Mrs Rivers. She's the headteacher, and the only one Fussy Forrest doesn't get to tell what to do.

'Today's baking challenge is spiced cinnamon and apple cake,' Mrs Tavella said. She switched on the whiteboard to show the recipe on-screen. 'Ingredients . . . what do we need to collect from the food cupboard?' she asked, rubbing her hands together.

'Flour, eggs, oil, brown sugar, cinnamon and apples!' we chorused.

'Perfect!' she crooned. 'And what do we do before we start cooking?' she prompted.

'Wash our hands!' we chanted.

'Wonderful!' she exclaimed as if we had just told her the answer to a really hard maths problem. Even Summer Singh, the moodiest member of the VIPs, smiled. Mrs Tavella was one of my favourite teachers – her enthusiasm for cooking was infectious. According to Mrs T, baking was a 'delicate balance of art and science'.

We split into pairs and got out all the dishes and ingredients. Each pair was to make one cake and then we would put our cake tin on one shelf in the oven and another pair would put their cake tin on the shelf below it. Naomie and Steph sat across from me and Charligh at our cookery bench. The Fabulous Four would share an oven.

'One more thing,' Mrs T said, 'the winner of the most delicious cake will get this.' She held up a glossy recipe book with colourful cupcakes pictured on the front cover.

'Who's judging?' called out Theo. He was Olly's cooking partner.

'I am,' Mrs T said, looking rather pleased at the idea of tasting all our cakes.

Rosie raised her hand to speak. 'Miss, my mum is a professional baker and she's been giving

34

me special one-to-one lessons in gourmet cake-making and now she says I'm nearly as good as her.'

I bit down on the laughter that wanted to spill out, remembering my promise to Ms Morgan.

Erica chimed in: 'Rosie makes the best cakes, miss.' I could tell she was lying because the tips of her ears went pink when she told fibs.

'What a surprise! How did we know Erica would say that?' Charligh said behind her hand.

I giggled, then tried to disguise it as a cough when Mrs T gave us a stern look.

'Thank you, ladies, for your contributions,' Mrs T said, not sounding very thankful at all. 'I'll be judging solely on what you bake today in this class. May the best baker win!'

I couldn't bear Rosie and Erica looking down their noses at us again. We were every bit as good as them and we had a decent chance of proving it right here in cooking class. The best thing about beating Rosie this way was that it wasn't breaking any rules.

Charligh and I got to work on our cake. After adding the cinnamon to the flour and sugar, we stirred the dry ingredients into our eggs, milk and oil mixture. Our batter was thick and smooth, and the wholewheat flour we were using gave it a warm brown colour.

I greased the side of the cake tin and lined it with baking paper. Charligh poured the cake mix in carefully until eventually the tin was filled.

We had sliced three apples thinly and all that was left to do was to arrange them over the top of the cake.

I took a stroll round the class, stopping at Rosie and Erica's bench. While our table looked like a flour bomb had exploded on it, theirs was sickeningly immaculate. I spotted sultanas dotted through their cake mixture.

Rosie caught me sneaking a look at the ingredients on her table and snatched them up, hiding the labels protectively. 'I know we're the best, but *pleeease* don't copy us. Excellence cannot be imitated,' she said. Then she flicked her hair at me.

'Don't flatter yourself. I was looking at the flour you've got all over your face,' I retorted, leaving Rosie to paw anxiously at her forehead.

I got back to our own bench, feeling a bit nervous. Their mixture did look good. 'Maybe we should have added our own twist, or a little more cinnamon,' I wondered aloud. I dabbed my finger gently into the mixture and tasted it. 'It could do with, you know . . . a little more kick.'

'We need to be finished by 3 p.m.,' Mrs Tavella called. 'So if you haven't already done so – it's time to put your cakes into the oven.'

Everyone started rushing around, while the VIPs calmly placed their cake tin in their oven.

Charligh shrugged. 'It's up to you, but we don't have much time left.'

I hurried over to the spice rack, where the spices were ordered alphabetically. A . . . B . . . C. I grabbed the jar of ground cinnamon and sprinkled a little more into the tin. Then I bunged the cake on the top rack of the oven, above Steph and Naomie's.

Thirty minutes later, our timer went off. Mrs T came over and supervised us while we took the cake out and set it on our cooling rack. I looked over at the VIPs' cake, which had been out for a few minutes now. It looked a bit flat and sad compared to ours. 'Look at our cake,' I crowed.

The cake stood rather majestically. It was golden brown and ever so perfectly crusty at the edges. Some of our classmates came over to peek at it. Even Zach looked impressed. He and Sebastian had managed to burn theirs.

'It probably tastes *dis-gus-ting*,' Rosie said confidently. She pushed through Zach and Sebastian to get a better look.

Charligh held up a butter knife, eased it into our cake and hacked out a generous slice. It sure smelled . . . spicy. I suddenly started to have doubts. Perhaps I'd overdone it with the cinnamon. But Mãe always said half of winning was about looking like a winner, so I put on my best confident smile and ripped off a piece of paper towel and slid the large slice on to it.

'Really? If I didn't know better, Rosie, I'd think you're afraid of the competition.' I thrust the cake at her. 'Why don't you try it, if you are so sure it's "dis-gus-ting",' I said, mimicking her.

'Afraid of the competition?' Erica said, tittering.

'Uh-oh, looks like we have an echo again,' said Charligh with a smirk.

'Do you think I really want to try anything you lot have made?' Rosie said, wrinkling her nose disdainfully.

I shrugged. 'You could just say if you're worried it will taste better,' I said.

Rosie scowled and took the slice of cake, then she ordered Erica to cut a slice of their cake for us to taste.

'I'm never afraid of you, Jaz!' Rosie said.

'It's a cake-off,' whooped Zach.

Mrs T was still helping other pairs get their cakes out of the oven so she didn't notice the small knot of pupils watching Rosie and me with interest.

Erica handed me the slice of their cake. I couldn't help thinking, although wild dragons wouldn't have made me say it out loud, that it smelled wonderful. I nibbled a little. Despite looking rather ordinary, it was quite nice. It wasn't mouth-wateringly, earth-shatteringly, life-changingly delicious, though. Not like ours would be.

'Um, it's OK,' I said. 'Go on, then – try ours. It will be lush. I promise you'll have never tasted a cake like it.'

'Whatever,' Rosie said, coughing a little. She must have caught a whiff of the spice too, but she took a large bite anyway. She wolfed it down, barely chewing it before swallowing hard. Within a few seconds, her eyes were shining, bulging with delight.

'Spit it out, then – what do you think?' I asked her.

Then I saw it. Her face was turning an unusual blend of grey and green. The shine in her eyes . . . it wasn't delight; it was queasiness. And then she really *did* spit it out. All over the paper towel.

'Ewww,' said Summer, holding her nose.

Rosie clasped her hands over her mouth. She clutched her stomach. Zach and the other boys guffawed loudly. I blushed. This was a bit much even by Rosie's standards. It was just like her to make a joke out of something we'd made and embarrass us! I narrowed my eyes as she continued her dramatics and theatrics.

'Mrs T is the judge anyway. The final decision is down her,' I said, feeling thoroughly exasperated.

Steph stepped forward. 'I don't think Rosie's joking,' she said grimly. 'Miss!' she shouted, waving Mrs Tavella over from the other side of the classroom. As the crowd surrounding us parted to make way for Mrs T, I heard a horrible retching sound and the air suddenly filled with a warm, bitter smell.

I froze, hardly daring to turn my head towards what I knew would be there. I edged back and held my breath before sneaking a look. Doubled over, Rosie was standing in a pool of her own sick. Some of it had managed to get all over Erica's arm, so she was looking pretty green now too and making retching sounds of her own as she headed towards the toilets.

Everyone groaned and backed off, horrified, holding their noses, while Rosie had a vengeful glint in her eyes. She straightened up a little.

'Jaz did it!' she croaked, pointing a limp finger at me. 'She's gone and poisoned me!'

4

The Spark

OK, OK. I get it, you think I'm the villain of the story, right? It isn't what it looks like, though. HONEST!

Later, when Mrs T nibbled a tiny edge of our cake to try to figure out what had made Rosie puke, she found out what the problem was. It was ... (drum roll, please) ... chilli powder! And although Mrs Tavella explained to Fussy Forrest, who had stormed in, that it was an easy mistake to make, since the spices were arranged alphabetically, Fussy Forrest didn't agree. She said that only somebody 'very stupid' could have mixed cinnamon up with extra-hot chilli powder, and that even if I wasn't completely stupid, I was 'a miscreant'. After checking on Rosie and Erica in the medical room, she frogmarched me and Charligh to her office.

'You have made Rosie and Erica sick, girls! I could have guessed *you* were at the bottom of this plot!' she roared. Spittle sprayed out with every syllable, and her face grew fiery puce.

I tried my best to calm her down. 'But people do it all the time, don't they?' I said. 'Substitute one spice for another? And it doesn't end up with people getting sent to the medical room, does it? Mrs Tavella calls it "culinary innovation",' I explained.

Well, I can tell you right now that my explanation didn't do one jot of good. In fact, it just made her face turn even redder. I should have known a dreadful bore like her wouldn't have understood culinary innovation.

'It was the smell of Rosie's sick that made Erica puke,' said Charligh. 'She didn't even try the cake. So, technically, Rosie is half responsible for the vomit pools,' she added reasonably.

A bulging vein on Mrs Forrest's forehead trembled dangerously as her eyes darted from me to Charligh and back to me, like a snake ready to pounce.

'Ms Morgan tells me you're on report this week, Jasmina. Your behaviour has already been terrible this term and we're only on week three! We really don't want a repeat of Year Five.' Fussy Forrest started listing a few entries from my rather long Year 5 crime sheet, including being late for her class most Mondays, accidentally smashing the window of the teachers' bike shelter with a football, and bursting into uncontrollable laughter during her speech at the special assembly for Year 1 pupils and their parents.

'And you, Charligh, are not much better,' she went on. 'But, looking at Jasmina's track record, it's not hard to figure out who the ringleader is here.' Fussy Forrest's mouth set itself in a straight line as she again spent several seconds looking from me, to Charligh, then back to me.

Finally, something like a smile played on her lips, as if she'd just had a really good idea. I was worried. A good idea for Fussy Forrest was always bad news for me.

'I'll be speaking to Ms Morgan shortly and I know she'll abide by my strong recommendation to exclude you from dance until after the holidays.'

I breathed in sharply. This was horrible! Worse than horrible. *Catastrophic*.

'That's not fair! We both made the cake,' protested Charligh. 'I know my rights.'

'Do you? How about the right to be banned from dance class along with Jasmina?'

Charligh folded her arms 'Fine, I quit,' she said.

'I'm sure the show will carry on perfectly well without the two of you,' declared Mrs Forrest with a smirk.

'But you don't understand, miss – we need to be in the dance showcase this year,' I squeaked.

Fussy Forrest glared at me. 'Not another word from either of you. It's home time now, so go home. NOW!' and she flung the door of her office open and pointed into the hallway.

I blinked away the tears that were prickling behind my eyes. Mrs Forrest was wrong about one thing, though. I *was* completely stupid. Why hadn't I paid more attention to what I was putting in the cake? It seemed like, no matter how hard I tried, I ended up ruining everything.

On Fridays, I went to Charligh's house for dinner after school, or she came to mine. Tonight, I was glad it was my turn to go to hers. Telling Mãe and Dad the bad news could wait until later. As late as possible. I chewed on the corner of my bottom lip. I could just imagine how the mood would sink in my house when I told them they wouldn't be watching me in the showcase after all. And then they'd argue about why it had happened or what could be done to fix it.

We sat on the rug in Charligh's front room with her twin baby brothers, Rory and Reuben, while Mrs Gorley made dinner. Charligh had found two old flowerpots. We drew round eyes and a big smile on them with marker pens, and stuck on thin black strips of paper decorated with blue glitter glue for the hair. Then we looped some string through holes in the rim. The twins laughed and clapped their hands in delight at our flowerpot characters.

It was always nice at Charligh's. The Gorleys were a bit like those happy families you see in movies and TV adverts. Once, when I mentioned to Charligh how horrid it was when parents argue so loud that your head hurts the next day, she looked totally blank. I never brought it up again. She wouldn't understand.

'Sorry I got us kicked out of dance club,' I said.

My best friend shrugged. 'You didn't get me kicked out. I left. No way was I going to dance without you,' she said. 'Plus, I was getting bored of it anyway. Next time I'm up on a stage, I'll be singing and acting. I'm much better at that than dancing.'

Charligh wanted to be a famous theatre actress when she was older. She was always practising different accents. One day it would be Cockney, the next she'd have a Yorkshire accent or a plummy posh one, but lately she had been trying out her American accents. She was mad about musicals like *Cats*, *Dreamgirls*, *The Lion King* and her favourite – *Hairspray*. Charligh had watched them a zillion times and knew all the words. For her tenth birthday, Mrs Gorley took me and Charligh to watch *Matilda the Musical* in London. Charligh wouldn't stop belting out 'When I Grow Up' on the train home, but all the passengers smiled at her because she had such an amazing singing voice – just like the stars in the West End shows!

She stuck her right hand in one of the pots. 'Hi, I'm Cherry the rock-star princess from California,' she said, putting on an American accent. She shook it from side to side, so it looked like a princess rocking out. Cherry's blue hair whipped out all over the place. Normally I would have laughed, but right now I couldn't even imagine smiling ever again.

'I wish I wasn't bothered about getting kicked out of dance, but I am,' I said, puffing out heavily.

Charligh kept rocking Cherry, much to the delight of the twins, who laughed loudly. 'Why do you even care so much, Jaz?'

I opened my mouth to try to explain but I forced the words back down. Lately some of my parents' rows had got so angry and loud they made me feel sick and sore all over. What if what had happened today set off another of their arguments? And now Mãe wouldn't get to see me star in the showcase. I'd failed everyone. Again. Charligh was my BBF but she hadn't understood the last time I'd said anything so she wouldn't understand this time.

I was saved by Mrs Gorley announcing dinner was ready. 'Bring the boys too, please,' she called.

At the dinner table, Charligh put Rory in a highchair beside their mum and I put Reuben in another one next to Mr Gorley. It had been an utterly horrid day, what with accidentally poisoning Rosie and being expelled from dance club, but the smell of freshly baked shepherd's pie made me feel so much better.

'Let's get stuck in!' said Mr Gorley cheerfully. I dug my fork into the creamy cheese and mash in front of me and opened my mouth wide –

Rrrrrng!

The doorbell buzzed long and shrill. I put my fork back down.

Mrs Gorley got up to answer it, there was brief murmuring, and then she came back in with a worried frown. My dad was trailing after her. He was looking unusually frazzled – and he was two hours early. Something was wrong. I just knew it. My stomach twisted itself into a knot.

'Don't panic, love,' he began, 'but . . . there's been a fire at the house.'

Fire! Fire!

'A fire?'

I shot up, bumping little Reuben's highchair. His cup crashed down, drowning his plastic bowl in apple juice.

'Mãe . . . Jordan . . .' I fumbled for the words as I rushed round the table to Dad.

'Calm down, Jaz. The firefighters are there now and everyone's safe. Not much harm has been done to the house. Jordan was at orchestra practice,' Dad said. His voice was as steady as ever, but his hand curled a little tighter on my shoulder. My stomach churned.

'What happened? Was Mãe in?' I asked.

'Yes, your mother was in, but she's absolutely fine. A little shaken but no harm done. Everyone's safe,' he repeated.

Charligh's mum and dad exchanged A Look. It was one of those looks grown-ups give each other, the sort they think kids can't see.

'You could always finish your dinner, stop here tonight and go home tomorrow morning. That would be lovely, wouldn't it, girls?' Mrs Gorley said brightly. Too b⸱⸱⸱

'Thank yo⸱⸱⸱ ⸱⸱⸱ome now if it's all the same, Mr⸱

'Are you s⸱⸱⸱ ⸱⸱⸱finish off your theatre perfor⸱⸱⸱ ⸱⸱⸱?' she coaxed.

I picked up m⸱⸱⸱ ⸱⸱⸱Thanks for having me,' I said politely but firmly.

'Thanks for helping, Viv,' Dad said as Mrs Gorley saw us out.

The ten-minute drive from Charligh's house on Orbit Drive to ours on Half Moon Lane felt much longer that day. Dad didn't say much.

He put on one of his radio stations that play Motown. He always sang or hummed along, but this time the happy Motown track rang out alone in the car.

I peered through the window as we pulled into our road. It was nothing like the horror story I'd conjured up in my mind. Everyone and everything looked absolutely fine. A group of firefighters stood chatting in our garden. One was crouching down, looking at something. As we got closer, I saw she was admiring the red-gold chrysanthemums and purple geraniums that lined the path to our front door. Mrs Chan, our next-door neighbour, was bringing out a tray of hot drinks for everyone. I unfastened my seat belt and clambered out. Dad was right after all: there had been nothing to worry about.

I weaved through the huddle of firefighters crowding our small front garden until I spotted Mãe. She'd drifted out a few metres away and was standing on the pavement. Her face was tight and pinched as she took a slow drag of her cigarette. She threw it down when she saw me and stamped on it, then she pulled me close to her. I snuggled into the soft blanket she had wrapped round her. 'Are you OK, Mãe?'

'Stupid *cigarros*! It was the *cigarro*,' she said. Mãe always mixed Portuguese with English, especially when she was stressed or excited.

'I was smoking in the back garden,' she explained, 'then I came in to check my phone and left the cigarette burning in the living room. Somehow I fell asleep and then the fire alarm woke me up.'

'Was anything burned?' I shivered.

She pulled me closer and smoothed my hair. 'No, nothing, apart from the pile of Dad's papers on the coffee table underneath the ashtray . . . The firefighters were very quick. The fire was also very quick – I couldn't have been asleep for more than five minutes.'

'Five minutes is all it takes for a house to catch fire, Iris!' Dad's voice came from behind us, sounding cold and distant. I'd never heard him speak to her like that. I shivered more and looked up at Mãe. She looked directly at Dad.

'*Desculpa!* Sorry! I apologize for not being perfect like you, Drew.' Her words shot out angrily. She didn't sound very sorry at all.

I stepped out of the line of fire, wondering if I was invisible to them. That's what I felt like. I clenched my fists; my nails dug into my skin.

The firefighters were beginning to climb back into their engines and the last of them were coming out of the house. One of them, a short, stocky man with a smiling, round face, coughed loudly.

'You've had a lucky escape, Mr and Mrs Campbell. Please be more careful in future. It's a good thing your smoke alarms were in perfect working order or the result could have been very different . . .' He hesitated and cleared his throat again. 'You have children. I understand that neither of them were here on this occasion, but if anything like this happens again we would have to report it to the relevant authorities.'

'Of course,' murmured Dad. I'd never seen him look so ashamed before. Not even when he was caught by Granny Campbell eating our Easter eggs, or when Aunty Bella called him out for cheating during Monopoly last Christmas.

Mãe nodded.

'Just make sure you leave the windows open to get the last of the smoke out,' he added. 'Have a good evening,' he said, and he hoisted himself into his fire engine.

'Did you hear what he just said?' Dad said as we walked back into the house.

'Of course,' Mãe replied. 'I have ears, don't I?'

Poor Mãe. I could tell how she felt. Dad didn't need to make her feel worse. It was the first time I'd seen Dad like this. His jaw was set and his arms were trembling.

When we finally got back in, I ran up the stairs, two at a time, speeding away from the fiery tensions below, half wishing I was one of the red engines roaring away down the street. I switched some music on and plugged in my earphones, hoping to drown out the bickering. After a while, I began to get worried about what I wasn't hearing so I switched the music off and opened my door a little. Silence. The only sound I could hear was my stomach rumbling furiously. I hadn't even managed to get a single forkful of shepherd's pie in my mouth at Charligh's before Dad had arrived.

I sat back down on my bed, leaving the door open, and looked at my phone. There was a message from Charligh.

R u OK? x

I replied straight away.

> Yeah, we are all OK. Super cool to
> have firefighters in my garden. I wish
> I'd taken a picture of the ladders. x

Charligh loved firefighters.

> I'm totally jealous of you right now.

I sighed. I was tired of pretending.

> Don't be . . .

My thumb hovered over the send button. I heard
quick steps come towards my door followed by a
sharp knock. I deleted what I wrote and started
again:

> Jordan's knocking on my door. Speak
> to you later x

Tell him I said hi :) Speak to you tmrw x

I opened the door for Jordan. He strode in and headed straight to the window, opening it a few inches so the cold evening air blew in.

'Come in and make yourself comfortable, Jordan,' I said sarcastically.

'Hey, did you close the windows, Jaz?' He frowned. 'Dad said we've to leave all of them open until we go to bed. We don't want to die of smoke inhalation.'

I rolled my eyes. I didn't know why Charligh thought my brother was so cool. Jordan was a total nerd. 'I can just die of pneumonia, then, right?'

'Don't worry,' he said.

'About?' I prompted.

He sat down on the floor under my window and crossed his legs. Jordan never came into my room lately. Not now he thought he was such a grown-up just because he was in Year 8.

'Let's play a game of Favourites,' he suggested. 'We haven't played that for a while.'

Actually, we hadn't played Favourites since *two* whole summers ago, when Jordan announced he was too old to play 'my baby game' any more, even though it was actually him who made it up when we were really little. Favourites is basically a speed quiz. One person asks something like, 'What's your favourite cake?' The other person has to reply instantly and then ask a different question, which has to be answered, and so on. If you hesitate for more than one second, you're out. We would keep a tally and it was the best of five games to be the winner.

So here was Jordan pretending like it was super normal for him to be sitting on my purple fluffy rug asking to play the 'baby game' he had refused to play for the past two years.

'OK, Jordan, we can play *your* baby game,' I said, not one to let an opportunity to gloat go by. 'I'll go first. What's your favourite ice-cream flavour?'

'Cookies and cream. Who's your favourite football player?'

'Rachel Yankey, obviously,' I said, rolling my eyes. I automatically glanced towards the wall where the giant poster of my favourite football star was. 'What's your favourite hobby, except for playing the viola and piano?'

'Music isn't my hobby, Jaz; it's my life,' Jordan said.

'You're not playing this game properly at all.' I yawned. 'This isn't the time for grand speeches about your life. Go and stand on a podium and find an audience for that.'

'You're too easy to wind up, baby sis.'

'I'm not a baby and I wish I wasn't your sister.'

'Really?' Jordan said. 'Do you think Dad will let me trade you in for another sister? One who doesn't leave her cheese-smelling football boots lying in the hallway?'

'Hey! My shoes don't smell like cheese,' I protested. 'But you do!'

'That's it,' said Jordan. He stood up and spread his fingers out, a serious look crossing his face. 'Tickle war.'

'Noooo!' I curled up into a ball, trying to protect the most ticklish part of me, which was the soles of my feet. Jordan wasn't even a little bit ticklish, so the tickle war was never actually much of a war. I giggled uncontrollably as his fingers came closer.

'I haven't even tickled you yet and you're giggling already!' he howled, doubling over.

I used this to my advantage and made a beeline for the door to escape him. I yanked it open and rushed out on to the landing, closely followed by Jordan. The harsh clatter of our parents' bickering bounced up the stairs.

'Let's go back in and play Favourites, then, Jaz,' he said, tugging at my sleeve. 'I promise to follow all the rules this time.'

I pulled my arm away. 'Shh, listen . . . can you hear it?' I said.

The roar had subsided to a tense whisper. They spoke quietly to each other in Portuguese. Dad spoke Scottish, which was basically like English but in a funny accent, where he said words like 'wee', which meant small, and pronounced 'Dad' like 'Da' when he spoke to my grandfather in Dundee. He'd spent a whole year living in Portugul, where he'd met Mãe, who had moved there from Angola. He learned to speak Portuguese, which is also Angola's national language.

I could only hear snatches of their conversation and my head was all muddled, so I was finding it hard to make any sense of the Portuguese. I knew a lot of Portuguese words, but only Jordan was truly bilingual and spoke both languages fluently. So as we listened I watched his face carefully to see his reaction.

'*Você mudou . . .*' You've changed . . .

'*Eu não posso pedir desculpa pela maneira que você me vê . . .*' I can't apologize for how you see me . . .

'*É tudo sempre sobre você . . .*' Always about you . . .

Jordan wasn't giving anything away, nor was his face.

Suddenly, there was a mighty thud, bang and a crash. My heart did a triple somersault. Mãe appeared in the hall and began storming up the stairs.

Jordan and I looked at each other.

'Come on, Jaz,' he said, walking back into my room.

This time, I followed him.

Broken Things

The next sounds we heard were even more terrible, and not even my closed door could block them out. It was Mãe on the phone. She was speaking low and fast in Portuguese, with shuddering sobs in between.

Eventually Jordan went back to his room and started playing some of his viola exercises, a little faster and louder than usual. I reckoned his brain and heart were probably racing as fast as mine.

Then the house became eerily silent for a long while and I wished he would play another piece.

I looked at the clock. It was 7 p.m., about an hour since Mãe had burst out of the living room. I was more on edge now than when they were actually yelling at each other. I pulled Kinsley, my stuffed elephant, down from the top bunk bed and hugged her. She used to be the mascot for Dad's team, the Bramrock Rangers, who were also known as the Reds, and she still wore her Reds scarf. I shivered and wrapped it round her again, although the one who was cold was me, not Kinsley.

I opened my door cautiously, hoping to hear something. Anything. Even the sound of them arguing. Mãe was right in front of me. Her eyes were red and swollen. How long had she been standing there?

'*Princesa* . . . please, come downstairs.'

My heart did another triple spin, landing in my stomach with a plop, as I followed Mãe silently down the stairs and into the living room. I sat on the sofa next to Jordan. Mãe took a seat across from me. My parents looked at each other.

Eventually, Dad spoke up. 'Your mum's going to spend some time at Aunty Bella's.'

'So? What's the big deal? Mãe stays over at *Tia's* all the time,' I said. I leaned back like I wasn't bothered, but I already knew. This was different. I could feel it. I could see it. Mãe's huge striped suitcase was sitting in the corner, and the air felt thick and rough like cardboard. My chest tightened.

'So when are you coming back?' I asked. 'Tomorrow? Or the day after that? Or the day after the day after tomorrow?' I rambled on, hoping if I kept on talking I wouldn't have to hear anything I didn't want to.

'I'll be away for a bit longer than a couple of days,' Mãe said.

'How long?'

'I'm not sure, sweetie,' she replied, her eyes not quite meeting mine.

I realized I'd been holding my breath. I let it out in one sharp go, but my voice still came out all strangled and high, like Mrs Chan's cat when her grandson grabbed its tail.

'You can't just go places and not know how long you're going to be away for,' I said. My throat hurt now too, along with my chest and my stomach and my heart. Everything was hurting.

Dad put the tips of his fingers together, making a diamond shape with his hands, and stared through them.

'I . . . we . . . aren't sure,' Mãe said softly. She stood up and the sound of her chair scraping across the wooden floor cut through the silence. 'Look after your sister, Jordan,' she said.

I sneaked a look at my big brother. He looked confused for a moment and he ran his hands through his short brown curls, but then he stood up straight with his shoulders squared and nodded seriously.

'Don't worry, I'll look after Jaz. Have a nice time with *Tia*.'

Have a nice time with Aunty? The ordinariness of my brother's words made me feel even queasier. *A nice time?* Didn't he get it? Mãe wasn't going away on a happy holiday. She was leaving us. Swapping Dad, Jordan and me for our Aunty Bella, who lived a whole half-hour drive from us in Brighton.

I looked at Dad. Why was he just letting it happen? There must be something we could say or do. Maybe we could lock the doors. Hide the car keys. Beg her to stay? Pretend I was sick? Just until tomorrow – until she saw sense again. Because all of this was a great big mistake.

I opened my mouth to say something, but instead I watched Mãe kiss me on the top of my head. I froze, feeling just as helpless as Dad seemed to be.

'You know,' she said, 'I'm just a phone call away. Anything you need, just ask me and I'll be there.'

Didn't she get it? It was *her* I needed, and I needed her here at home. She gave Jordan a quick hug and headed out of the door. Part of me felt she was leaving because she'd realized that I'd not only failed to get the lead part in *Spinning Alices* but I wasn't even good enough to be in Ms Morgan's dance club. Stupid, I know, because she couldn't have known any of that already, but although my head told me it wasn't my fault, deep inside I had the faint, uncomfortable feeling that some of it really was. Maybe she'd always known I'd never been good enough and this was just the final confirmation she'd been waiting for. I was a troublemaker, a failure, and I ruined everything.

'Watch your feet, Jaz. Your mãe knocked it over by accident earlier.' My eyes followed to where Dad's finger was pointing. He was gesturing at the fragments and splinters of our beautiful cornflower-blue vase, the one our family had made together on holiday in Turkey.

7

Stuck in the Mud

That Saturday morning, the whole house smelled of happy family breakfasts. Except today Jordan had left early for his all-day music workshop, so it was just Dad, me and a mum-sized gap. Dad had laid stacks of banana pancakes on the breakfast bar. He poured himself a glass of orange juice and sat down beside me.

If you look up the phrase 'morning person' in the dictionary, it wouldn't surprise me if you'd find a picture of my dad. Today, though, his sandy-brown hair stood up in about a zillion different directions and his pale skin had a dull grey tinge to it.

'Morning, princess,' he said. His brow was furrowed. A thread of worry pulled inside me. I wondered whether he was thinking about Mãe.

'Are you late for dance again?' he asked.

'Um, no. I kind of quit that,' I said casually. I hoped that Ms Morgan wasn't on the phone to Mãe right now, telling her exactly why she wouldn't need to make me a costume for *Spinning Alices*. 'I'll find another club to join.'

Luckily for me, Dad had other things on his mind. 'That's nice, Jaz,' he said vaguely. I didn't know whether to be relieved or sad as I watched Dad glide over to the sink and rinse his glass under the hot tap without another word about dance. He let the tap run for ages, long after he'd finished washing his glass. 'I'm going to get on with the housework, pet,' he said. 'I think this house needs a spring clean.' He got down on his knees in front of the cupboard under the sink and started pulling out bleaches and cleaning sprays.

I felt terrible and didn't know who to talk to. *Not Dad anyway*, I thought as I trudged back up the stairs and into my bedroom. I'd just make things worse for him. I decided to message Charligh.

She soon replied.

> What could be worse than your house
> nearly going up in flames?

> Your mum leaving?

> No way! That is THE WORST. Are you
> OK, Jaz? Do you want to come round?

> No, I'm OK, thanks. She'll come back . . .
> She has to.

> Are you sure? We can sing all the songs
> in *Hairspray* and I might even let you
> have the mic this time . . . well, maybe.

> I'm fine. Honest.

It was sweet that my BBF always tried to cheer me up, but right now I didn't feel like talking about it or watching her sing along to musicals. I knew what I did feel like, though. I changed into my grey leggings and pulled on a sky-blue hoodie before heading back down to the kitchen.

Dad was hard at work, wiping down the inside of the windows. He pretended to mop sweat from his forehead when he saw me. 'This is some workout,' he said, and he gave a fake sort of laugh, which was much worse than him not laughing at all.

'Dad, is it OK if I go down to the common?' I knew I'd find the Year 6 boys playing football. Running down a pitch with a ball at my feet always helped me forget about all the bad stuff.

'Sure.' He looked at the clock. 'Make sure you're back by two, OK?'

I nodded as I left the room, taking my neon purple cycle helmet off the side table as I headed out.

When I reached the common, I propped my bike up against a tree and clipped my helmet to the crossbar.

'Hey,' I called out to Theo, who was making teams from the large group of boys standing on the damp grass. As usual, I was the only girl, but playing football with the horrid Year 6 boys was better than nothing. 'Count me in!'

'Sorry,' Theo said, looking guilty. 'We've started practising for the tournament, so it's only the ones who've made it on to the school team that can play in this game.' He stole a sideways look at Zach, who gave him a thumbs up. He was talking about the annual local Bramrock schools football tournament, which was played by teams of Year 5 and Year 6 kids.

My jaw clenched in anger. That wasn't fair! The only reason I hadn't made the team was because the tournament had always been limited to boys only. And Rotten Roundtree, who was on the official tournament committee, said he didn't see why that should change now. Still, last year, the boys had let me join in their team practice games. It was just that Zach didn't want me to play, because this year, after practising all summer, I was dribbling rings round him and his mates.

'Go play with the girls,' Sebastian called.

'The girls don't like playing football. Why else would I want to play with you boys?' I said, hands on hips.

'Not true. Look at Naomie – she'd make a great defender. We saw the way she headed that gummy bear,' Zach taunted.

Sebastian guffawed loudly.

Now they were just making me angry.

'Don't be bitter because Naomie thinks you're all gross. Especially you, Bacon Boy.'

Zach Bacon, the bully boy of Bramrock, scowled and gestured with his thumb to the side of the field. 'Get lost, Jaz.'

I hated the way he looked so smug with his foot resting comfortably on the ball – the ball those horrid boys weren't going to let me play with. I took an angry swipe at it, but instead of making a brilliant kick I slipped on the wet grass and started to slide. I waved my arms about, desperately trying to stay on my feet.

Plop!

I landed on my bum, hitting the muddy grass with a squelch. The cold, slimy mud seeped through my light-grey leggings and on to my skin.

The boys laughed uncontrollably. Even Olly tittered a little. My face flushed so hot you could have fried an egg on it. I stood up with as much dignity as a cold, wet, muddy mess of sludge could muster and walked off.

Back home, I tried to creep back in quietly, but I tripped over the shoes left out in the hall so ended up making an awful racket. I wanted to cry with frustration. I couldn't do anything right that morning! Dad poked his head out from the living room. He was holding a mop. When he saw me, his eyes widened.

'Ms Morgan called,' he said. 'I think we'd better have a chat, Jaz, but first you need to get changed. I'll make us both a cup of minty hot chocolate – just the way you like it. Then we'll talk about everything, OK?'

I nodded. My eyes brimmed with tears and I kept my head very still so they wouldn't tip out as I walked up the stairs. Dad didn't seem cross. In fact, he was being as kind as ever, and that's what made it worse. He'd got enough to deal with, and so did Mãe. Whatever was she going to think when Dad told her the real reason I'd taken a break from dance?

I showered all the mud and grass off me and changed into some clean clothes. I felt better already. As promised, Dad had made two lovely steaming mugs of hot chocolate. I curled my legs up on the sofa.

'Your dance teacher was actually calling to speak to your mum about the costumes,' Dad began, 'and then she mentioned something about cakes? And making another student sick? It seemed almost unbelievable and didn't make much sense, but then she had to get off the phone to attend to the class.'

I sighed, feeling defeated. 'Rosie's gone and ruined everything for me.'

'So it didn't happen?' Dad asked.

'Well, it did,' I admitted, 'but not in the way they'd have told the story. It . . . it was an accident. Honest.' I took a deep breath and told Dad everything. I could tell he was still sad about Mãe leaving, because he didn't so much as smile when I got to the part about Rosie and Erica chucking up and making a mess everywhere.

'It's Ms Morgan's loss, if you ask me,' Dad said kindly. 'Oh, I meant to say – Jordan's at Aunty Bella's until tomorrow lunchtime. He's staying overnight because he has an orchestra recital again in Brighton tomorrow morning. She said you can stay too. I can drop you off in a couple of hours if you want.'

I shook my head. I was hoping that if I didn't go over there, Mãe would have to come home, but also I didn't want to leave Dad. Not tonight.

'I'll go another time, Dad. I need to go to the library tomorrow,' I said.

I think we both felt a little sad our family was split in two this weekend. So, to cheer ourselves up, we played a football video game and I had fun building my dream team. I had Lionel Messi, Marcus Rashford and Harry Kane playing up front. Dad created a solid defence with Sergio Ramos, Gareth Southgate and Sol Campbell in the back with the legendary former England player David Seaman in goal. I tried to let Dad win to make him feel better. It seems he had the same idea, because in the final minute he let the slowest wobbly goal in, making the final score 1–0. *That didn't really go to plan*, I thought, sighing inside.

By then my stomach was gurgling. Dad laughed.

'I can hear your stomach rumbling,' he said. 'I think it's pizza-making time, don't you?'

I grinned. I had made Dad smile *and* he was going to make pizza! Dad's the Greatest Pizza Maker in the World, by the way. I scrolled through my mental menu of his best creations. My top three were Seafood Supreme, Tropical Fiesta and (my ultimate favourite) Rooster Royale, but today I knew which one I'd go for.

'Dad's Special, please!'

Dad gave a nod of approval. 'Ah, the timeless classic.' Dad's Special had all my dad's favourite toppings: red onions, sun-dried tomatoes, sweet peppers, mushrooms, all with a tangy tomato sauce on a thin crust.

After we'd washed our hands, he put all the ingredients for the dough into a large steel mixing bowl ready for me to knead and flatten. I loved getting rid of all the lumps and bumps and smoothing it down.

Once we'd finished with that bit, we put all the toppings on and Dad slid it into the oven.

'Now that's what I call teamwork,' he declared. He looked a bit happier now. 'Don't you wish that life was like making pizza?' he asked.

'What do you mean, Dad?'

'Well . . . we get the ingredients ready, then we roll it, shape it the way we want, bung it in the oven and finally wait for it to come out all ready and perfect for us. Imagine if life were like that. Why can't it be that easy, I wonder.' He looked as if he was talking to himself more than me, so I stayed quiet.

Anyway, I didn't have the answer, but I wished I did.

8

A Library Full of Surprises

I sat on the cushioned window seat at Bramrock Library and started reading *Little Women*. It was one of my most favourite books ever and I had a copy of it at home, but I liked to reread it when I was worried about something. It was comforting reading a story when you knew just how it was going to turn out.

I was already on Chapter 5 when my phone beeped. It was a message from Charligh.

Where are you? xx

I'm at the library. Do you want to come too?

We can get hot chocolate from the cafe?

As long as you don't force me to read anything. Mum said she can drop me off. See you in 20 minutes.

OK xx

I put *Little Women* back, then walked up the spiral stairs to the Hungry Readers cafe. I grabbed a table in the corner near the noticeboard. A staff member was looking annoyed as she tried to sort out the noticeboard wall. Stacks of flyers lay on the floor and she was trying to jam them into the holders.

I tried extra hard not to, but a giggle escaped my mouth. The girl was even worse at organizing things than me.

'Am I amusing you?' She turned round, catching me by surprise. The crystal stud in her nose twinkled at me, but her grey eyes didn't. I knew most of the staff at the library and the cafe but I'd never seen this girl before. *She must be new*, I thought. She had waist-length hair and she wore coral pink eyeshadow and bold black eyeliner that stretched just past the outer corners of her eyes in a perfect flick on each side of her face. Her badge told me her name was Rhiannon.

Meanwhile, behind her, a queue had built up. A man at the front with a green Mohican drummed impatiently on the counter and suddenly I felt sorry for Rhiannon. She was a bit grumpy, but I knew what it was like to feel everything was piling up on top of you.

'Why don't I sort out this noticeboard and you sort out the customers?' I offered, ignoring her question.

'And why would you want to do that?' she said, hands on hips.

By now, Peter, the old man who was always in the cafe, was rattling his stick impatiently against the floor. Together with Green Hair's drumming, they made quite an angry orchestra.

'To stop this awful racket?' I suggested.

Rhiannon nodded, a warm smile finally melting her icy stare. 'Thanks, kid.'

'My name's Jaz, actually,' I said.

'OK, Jaz Actually, I owe you one.' She grinned and thrust the rest of the leaflets into my arms. Within a few strides of her long legs, she was back behind the counter.

I sorted all the leaflets into different piles on the table, putting all the activities for the under-fives in one, then the childminding services in another, the tutors offering private lessons or classes at Bramrock College together in another – until everything was either neatly pinned up on the noticeboard or filed away in the plastic holders.

Eventually I was down to the last two flyers. One of them was for a fundraising walk that had happened two months ago, so I screwed that up into a ball and lobbed it into the waste-paper bin. Someone had ripped a chunk out of the other flyer and the bit that was left was stained on the back with brown marks, as if it had been used as a coffee-cup coaster. It was about to get scrunched up into a ball too, but before it ended up in the same bin, I noticed that on the ripped side there was the faint edge of a football. I squinted at the faded print on the flyer:

* * *

Brighton Girls' Under-11s Seven-a-Side
Football Tournament
League and non-league teams welcome!
Closing date for entries 7 October

* * *

There was a link to a website run by the Brighton Ladies' and Girls' Association, where you could find out more details. I inhaled sharply. Finally, a girls' football tournament that was open to primary schools in Bramrock! All the other ones I'd heard of were for secondary-school students or were in faraway places like Cornwall or London or Liverpool.

I pulled out my phone and typed in the web address, which took me to a website filled with images of women and girls playing football. I scrolled down and clicked on a picture of the poster, which took me to a form to enter the tournament. I stared at the screen, still holding my breath and the tatty bit of paper that just a minute ago I'd planned to chuck in the bin. Now I clutched it tight, as if my entire world depended on it.

And maybe it did. Football was the only thing I had ever really been any good at. I was tired of getting into trouble all the time, feeling like a klutzy kangaroo in dance and getting left out of school football. Perhaps I wasn't meant to be a star onstage, but maybe I could be a star on the football pitch? I imagined myself running down the wing, weaving in and out of my opponents, then curling the ball in. And this was not just any football tournament – this one was sponsored by Brighton and Hove Albion WFC. Imagine that – a real football team who played in the Women's Super League!

'What's that?' Charligh said as she burst into the cafe and sank down into the seat opposite me. She was wearing huge sunglasses that I was sure she'd borrowed from her mum.

I gave her a questioning look.

'I'm practising for when I reach celebrity status,' she said in a hushed tone.

I decided not to point out that she was drawing more attention to herself by wearing sunglasses indoors in Bramrock on a grey day. And if the glasses didn't do it, the canary-yellow hairband tied in a huge bow certainly would.

'Look,' I said, pushing the flyer across the table to her.

'Eww . . . are those coffee stains on that scrap of paper, or something worse?'

'Never mind the coffee stains. It's a competition – a girls' football tournament. If we pull together a team, who knows, we could win this!'

Ignoring her loud yawn, I began to explain how the tournament would work. We would play at least three games against other teams, and each game would be thirty minutes – fifteen minutes each half. All we needed to do was enter online and provide the details of an adult supervisor for the team.

Charligh started to zone out, the way she did when I talked to her about the books I was reading.

'Well, what do you think?' I asked her eagerly.

'About what?' she said.

I blew out heavily. 'About starting our own football team!'

'Um . . . Jaz – why would I or any of the girls in our class be interested in a crusty old football competition?'

I pulled up the website on my phone. I flipped it round, so she could see what it said underneath the prizes tab:

1ST PRIZE

£250 worth of sports equipment

Your name in the *Brighton Chronicle*

Medals presented by the mayor

In addition, the winning team will receive

the inaugural Brighton Girls'

Under-11s Seven-a-Side

Football Tournament trophy

'Think about it, Charligh,' I urged. 'We'd be almost famous. And can you imagine the look on the boys' faces when we win?' I added.

A bright smile spread across my best friend's face. She whipped off her sunglasses and her brilliant blue eyes sparkled like they had stars in them. I knew all I had to do was mention fame to Charligh and I'd get her attention!

'We get to be famous? *And* annoy the Year Six boys? Count me in!'

I tingled all over with excitement. My football dream was already becoming real. I'd recruited my first member of the team!

Up in my room, I sat cross-legged on the top bunk. My room was the best present I'd ever had. We'd decorated it a week before my tenth birthday. Mãe had painted the walls a rich, deep purple with black half-moon stencils round the edges. Dad had fixed 'floating' black glass bookshelves round the walls to hold all my favourite books. And Jordan and I had stuck the glow-in-the-dark purple stars on my ceiling.

As I sat on my bed, I squeezed a mini football and stared at the poster of Rachel Yankey, hoping to get inspiration. Yankey's eyes were firmly fixed on the ball and her right leg stretched back ready to strike.

Half the girls in my class didn't like PE and they completely detested football. I'm sure most of that was down to how rough the boys were when any of us girls dared to step on to the football pitch, and how they used to think it was funny to kick the ball at girls standing on the side. The boys had ruined football, just like they ruined a lot of things. Lipgloss, shopping, pizza parties, nail polish, movie nights . . . that's what most of the girls in my class seemed to prefer. What did any of that have to do with football, though?

I spun the ball right up in the air, and it came back down and landed neatly on my head, where I balanced it. I could hear the crowd cheer. Suddenly, I knew exactly what I could do to convince the other girls! All I needed was for Dad to say yes.

9

Team Selection

'Dad, I need a sleepover. An emergency sleepover.'

Dad's face went a bit pink, and he rubbed his nose for a long time. He always did that when he was trying not to laugh.

I gave him A Look. 'Dad, I'm serious.'

'How many people are you going to invite?'

'Hmm . . . nine . . .?' I said.

'*How* many? Nine girls plus you is ten!' He wasn't laughing now. He looked a bit scared, actually. 'How about we compromise: you can invite six. Deal?' He stretched out his hand.

'Deal,' I said, shaking Dad's hand. I grinned inside. I'll let you in on a secret – six was exactly the number of invites I needed to make. I'd listened to Mãe's advice: *Always ask for more than you want, so when you have to bargain down you're still happy*!

I typed out the invitation on Dad's laptop, using a fancy, swirly font, and printed out six copies of it. Next, I cut round them to make a hexagon shape. Then I put my signature at the bottom with a string of kisses.

It was just after 7 p.m. and it was getting dark. There was no way Dad would let me go out at this time by myself, but I just couldn't wait until tomorrow! I knocked on Jordan's door and asked him if he would come with me.

'Why don't you just text or email everyone?' he said, shrugging.

'Not everyone has a phone or email account, you know, Jordan. Plus, I need to stand out and be convincing. We had a lesson on persuasive communication last week. Miss Williams said "be personal and unique".'

Jordan snapped his fingers as if he'd just had a great idea. 'Hey! How about pigeon carrier, smoke signals or even Morse code? Those must be really unique nowadays.'

'Are you going to help me or not?' I demanded.

'OK, OK, I suppose I could do with a break from music practice.' He grabbed his jacket, which was hanging on the door. 'Ready?'

I grinned. 'Ready.'

The warm autumn breeze unsettled the piles of rust-coloured leaves gathered at the bottom of the trees. I tightened my cream woolly scarf round my neck and increased the speed of my small steps to keep up with Jordan's big strides. We headed up Half Moon Lane towards Naomie's on Crescent Avenue. I knew she'd be out (she usually had piano and saxophone lessons on a Sunday night), and the rest of her family didn't seem to be in either, so we pushed her invitation through the letter box.

Next up on the guest list was Steph. She lived at the end of the same street. Her family were definitely in – the sounds of her playful younger siblings spilled out from an open window. The door swung open to Kenny, who was Steph's stepdad. He had a big bushy beard and worked as an engineer on the oil rigs, drilling for oil in seas around the country. I had never seen much of him because he worked away for two weeks at a time or even longer before coming home for a break from his long shifts. He slept a lot when he was back, but he always had a quiet, kind smile when I saw him.

'You're one of Steph's lot, aren't you?' he said, leaning against the door frame. 'I'll call her for you – *Steph*! Your friend's here.'

'Hi, Jaz!' said Steph, appearing from the kitchen. 'Oh, and hi, Jordan. How are you?' She looked at me curiously, pulling off her thick green gardening gloves. 'I wasn't expecting you to call round,' she added. Steph was the most organized person in the world and she planned everything in advance. 'I was just taking the food scraps and old teabags out to the compost heap.' Steph's mum usually had her hands full with her little brothers, so Steph took care of their garden including filling up the compost bin every evening after dinner. She was really good at all that gardening stuff and she loved it too. Last year she'd won a Bramrock Green Award because of how she helped run a gardening club with a community group to develop the school's nature garden.

I pulled out her invitation and handed it to her.

'Let me know if you can make it,' I said as Jordan and I hurried back down the path. 'Dad's expecting us back soon and we've got one more house to go to!'

It was getting late now. Charligh must have been looking out of the window because before we even rang the bell she threw the front door open. She was wearing a baby-pink cowboy hat that hung at the back of her head from a string. That meant she had probably been practising what she called her Texas accent.

'Howdy, folks,' she drawled, fixing Jordan with a bright smile as if I, her best friend, had suddenly become invisible. Unfortunately, unlike Steph, my BBF wasn't so sensible. She thought my brother was cute. Super gross, right?

I handed her the invitation.

'Sure, I'll be there,' she said sweetly, switching to her normal accent. She looked at Jordan while she spoke, as if it was my brother who had invited her.

I rolled my eyes. 'We need to go, Charligh. Text me tonight, yeah?'

Within a few minutes of getting back to the house, the text alerts started to come through from the Fabulous Four. Steph was in and, of course, so was Charligh. About half an hour later, I got a reply from Naomie, who had just finished her music lessons – it was a yes from her too! I breathed a sigh of relief. Three yeses for my sleepover and, including me, that made four. I needed at least seven players for the team, so four wasn't quite enough yet, but it was getting there. There would have to be a few more at my football sleepover, and I knew exactly who to ask tomorrow at school . . .

I found Talia Janowicz alone in the nature garden during morning break. She was sitting quietly on the wooden mushroom stool next to the gooseberry shrubs and tall lavender plants. She had a tiny electronic chess set on her lap and looked as if she was trying to figure out her next move. I didn't know her very well – I don't think anyone knew Talia really well, to be honest – but she was the only other girl in my class who had joined in sometimes during football. She'd stopped playing halfway through Year 5 when Zach blocked her belter of a shot at goal with a handball and then lied about it. She'd just walked off without a word and never played again. I think she got really annoyed when people didn't play by the rules.

'Hi, Talia, I've been looking for you!' I said.

'How did you know I was here?' she asked.

I thought it was kind of weird that she only asked how I knew where to find her and not *why* I was looking for her, but then everyone knew Talia was a bit different. I don't mean that in a bad way. It's just that everyone knew she seemed to like being alone.

'I see you slip off sometimes to water the plants,' I replied.

She didn't say anything. Talia had chin-length light-brown hair which had a perfectly straight, blunt fringe that looked as if someone had styled her hair using a bowl.

'It's nice and quiet here,' I said, a bit flustered.

Talia wasn't at all flustered. She was super comfortable with silence, which I was a bit jealous of. I held out the invitation. She opened it carefully.

Mrs Forrest called Talia's work meticulous and said we should all be more like her. I hadn't been sure exactly what 'meticulous' meant, but Dad said it was when someone pays a lot of attention to detail, so basically it means fussy.

Talia's lips moved silently as her eyes glided along the page. 'Thanks. I will be there,' she said. She turned back to her chess set as if the conversation was over, and – just like that – it was.

I loped back over to the main playground to find the K triplets. They were playing by the soft climbing frame.

'Hi,' I said.

'Hi, Jaz,' Katy, Karina and Keeley chorused back.

I told them about the football sleepover party. Katy seemed interested, but Karina said their big cousin was taking them to the cinema that night.

'Plus, Keeley still has a funny heartbeat, remember? So Mum says we have to take it easy with doing other sports outside of dance,' said Karina. She was the oldest by four minutes and she never let the other two forget it.

I nodded. Keeley had had to spend a lot of time having operations in hospital when we were in infants. She said, when the triplets were born, the other two had taken up most of the oxygen in their mother's womb, so they ended up with healthy hearts, while Keeley's was a little weaker. She'd only started dance last year.

'Maybe another time,' Keeley said, looking apologetically at her sisters. 'I've got my final check-up at Great Ormond Street next year. The doctors might say my heart is strong enough now.'

'Anyway, we're so busy with dance. We don't mind missing out on this, Keeley, honest,' Karina said loyally. 'And we do everything together.'

'Why don't you ask Allie Norton?' Katy suggested, pointing over to the picnic tables where Allie was sitting with Layla Hussani. 'She's the best at netball in Year Five, and that is kind of like football except you use your hands . . . right?'

Wrong, I thought. Katy and her sisters turned and got on the climbing frame.

OK . . . I know I'm hardly going to win any Model Student of the Year awards, but Allie Norton had the reputation of spending even more time in Fussy Forrest's office than I did. She had a bit of a temper and a permanent scowl. Her best (and only) friend, Layla, was the complete opposite: she loved all things pink and sparkly, and right now she was scribbling in a notepad while Allie drummed at the edge of the playground table with a stick. They were both in Year 5 too, so I didn't know very much more about them.

'Hey!' I plopped down across from them. 'What are you writing?' I asked Layla.

'Poetry,' she said shyly, covering her paper with her elbow.

'Cool. Well, I'm having a sleepover this Saturday. A football party. If you can't make it, that's OK, but I would *reeeeally* love it if you could –'

That got Allie's attention. I guessed she probably didn't get invited anywhere by anyone because of her temper.

'Are you kidding?' said Allie.

'We'll be there!' Layla said quickly.

Pushing the invitations across the table, I tingled all over with excitement. I hadn't actually meant to invite Layla as well – I didn't think it would have been her thing – but I was happy to have her come too. In any case, I wasn't sure

I could handle Allie without Layla there to calm her down.

'How did it go?' asked Charligh as I took my seat after break time, ready for our weekly music lesson with Mr Webb, the peripatetic teacher.

I gave her the thumbs up. 'Perfect! Everyone's in. Me, you, Naomie, Steph, Talia –'

I was interrupted by a loud snort. 'What's that? Is that a list of all the losers in a new gang you've formed?' It was Rosie. She was at the table next to ours and she was leaning towards me.

'If you want to find losers in the school, you only need to take you and your robot crew to the toilets and look in the mirror,' Charligh retorted.

Mr Webb shot a warning look in our direction.

'Who cares about her?' I said. 'We've got way more important things to plan for this weekend.'

Rosie pulled a horrid face. She leaned in further but toppled right over.

'Rosie, stop messing around – and keep four legs on the floor. Remember: no swinging on seats!' Mr Webb said.

Rosie, her face fire-engine red, clambered back on to her stool with the help of Erica and Summer, as the entire class laughed.

Charligh grinned at me and turned back round from Rosie's literal downfall behind us. 'More important things?' she echoed. 'We sure do!'

Party Time

The following Saturday morning, I jumped out of bed and pulled open my lilac curtains. The sky was powdery blue dotted with grey cotton clouds but the sun was peeking out cautiously.

'First things first,' Dad said as I came downstairs to the wonderful smell of freshly fried French toast and turkey bacon. 'Breakfast, then shopping, a bit of cleaning – then let's get the snacks ready for your party!'

After an early lunch, we were all set. The snacks were ready, there was space for the sleeping bags in my room and Jordan was hiding safely up in his with his headphones on. All that was left was for me to get changed. I pulled on my jeans and a chunky-knit rust-coloured jumper. As a final touch, I applied some face oil, which made my brown skin and chestnut eyes glow warmly.

Ding-dong! the doorbell sang. The first guest had arrived!

I bubbled over with a mixture of excitement and nerves as I turned away from the mirror. This wasn't just any old sleepover. I had to make this the best one EVER so they would all see how much fun football could be. Bounding down the stairs two at a time, I arrived at the bottom and yanked the front door open.

It was Steph. Her face was flushed and she wobbled slightly before clutching at the door frame with both hands to steady herself.

'Mum and Kenny were busy with the little ones, so I used my own wheels,' she said brightly. She bent down to unclasp the straps on her rollerblades.

'New helmet?' I said, looking at her white helmet with teddy bear designs.

Steph shrugged as she pulled it off her head. Her dark-blonde hair usually hung down her back in a long plait. Today she had styled it in a pretty French braid. 'One of my little brothers was wearing mine while the other two tapped his head with wooden spoons. I had to use my old one. I haven't worn it since Year Four!'

She stepped inside, barefooted, holding a rollerblade in each hand.

'Don't worry,' she said, following me into the living room. 'I didn't forget my trainers. They're in my backpack.'

The wooden coffee table was crammed with snacks. Popcorn and banana chips. Apple, carrot and celery slices with a creamy dip. And cheese, crackers and grapes.

'Mmm ... my favourite,' said Steph. She plopped herself down on a chair and picked some celery slices from the spread. Steph always started with the vegetables.

Next to arrive was Talia. She looked a bit awkward at first, but thankfully Steph soon made her feel welcome by talking about chess with her. Then Layla's mum dropped Allie and Layla off. Allie was sporting her usual: red tracksuit and navy blue trainers. Layla wore a pink tartan skirt, a fluffy black jumper and a matching pink-and-black beret with sparkly black-patent loafers.

Charligh rushed in, wearing a cornflower-blue polka-dotted dress that flared out from the waist.

'Love the dress,' said Layla admiringly.

'It's vintage, darling!' said Charligh in her Posh Lady of the Manor accent.

Soon everyone was sitting around, enjoying the snacks. Dad and I had laid cushions out across the floor, and there were the armchairs and the long, comfy L-shaped couch to sit on too.

'You said there were going to be seven altogether. Who's missing?' Talia said. I told you she always paid a lot of attention to detail.

As if on cue, the doorbell rang, and Dad ushered Naomie in. She was wearing black jeans, a long top and cherry-red lace-up boots. I didn't usually see her at the weekends so I'd forgotten she only wore her glasses in school.

'Sorry I'm late,' she said.

I hugged her. 'I'm just glad you could make it at all.' Naomie had the busiest schedule ever; in between piano and saxophone lessons, she'd had extra tuition on Saturday mornings since she was on the school's Excellence in STEAM program-me. And, just so you know, it has nothing to do with trains. STEAM stands for Science, Technology, Arts, Engineering and Maths.

'Grab your snacks and sit back – it's movie time!' I announced.

I rolled down the blinds so it was all dark, while my friends helped themselves to some more food and settled into the cushions.

'*Flo's Football Fame*,' read Talia as I clicked on the film I'd got ready earlier. Layla and Naomie wrinkled their noses in apparent distaste at my movie choice.

'We can watch *Hairspray* later,' I said, and everyone cheered. 'Later,' I emphasized.

I hit the play button and squashed myself into the gap next to Charligh.

Flo's Football Fame was about the super-talented Florrie Redford who played for one of the first women's football teams in Lancashire back in the olden days. Not the 1980s or 1990s, but the *really* olden days – you know, way back when people had daft ideas about what women should and shouldn't do? It had sad parts as well as funny bits, and a big twist at the end to make a surprising but happy ending. It was based on the story of Lily Parr who played for the Dick, Kerr's Ladies, which was set up in 1917. In the closing scene, when Flo lifted the trophy and all her village came out to support her, my friends cheered and clapped.

I grinned. That had gone better than expected. Everyone was engrossed in the movie.

'Imagine people saying those women couldn't play football just because they weren't men!' Charligh said indignantly.

'I'm glad I don't live in the olden days,' said Talia with a frown.

'You still get people saying things like that nowadays, though,' Layla pointed out. 'My mum said it's called being sexist.'

'That's what my Uncle Gavin is . . . sexist,' said Allie. 'He said I couldn't be a builder when I told him I wanted to train to be one when I grew up. I'm not afraid of heights and I'm good with my hands, so I can if I want to.' She looked quite cross.

'We can all be anything we want to,' said Steph firmly.

'Exactly,' I chimed in. 'And there's lots of

professional women football players all around the world. In England, there's been a Women's Super League since 2010 and it has twelve teams. One of them's not far from us! They're called Brighton and Hove Albion WFC and they play at Crawley in the Broadfield Stadium. They might not be as famous or well paid as the men players, but women footballers are every bit as good.'

We all fell silent as we watched the rest of the credits roll up on the widescreen TV.

'It's Ice Factory time!' Charligh burst out at the end of the credits. Layla giggled. Trust Charligh to break up a quiet moment like this with her loudness, but she did have a point – it really was time for Ice Factory!

'What's that?' asked Talia.

'Follow me,' I said, walking through the door that led straight into the kitchen.

'It's the best thing ever!' Steph declared. 'We take out all of the tubs of ice cream from Jaz's freezer and raid the cupboards for toppings. Then we all take our places, like here, there, and there –' She pointed at different parts of the kitchen. 'For example, I stand at that side and put little sweets on, then I pass to you and you do the chocolate drops, then you pass the bowl to whoever's next in line who can put on fruit, and then the next person the sprinkles, and we go down the line until everyone's had a chance to put their topping on.'

'That sounds great,' Allie spluttered.

'It *tastes* even better,' Naomie said.

We spread out around the kitchen. Charligh and I pulled out all the toppings from the baking cupboard: sprinkles, edible silver balls, sugared jellies. Talia and Steph rummaged around in the fridge.

'Squirty cream, sliced melon, strawberries, honey, chocolate sauce,' Talia listed as she passed the items out one by one to Steph.

'Vanilla, chocolate fudge, cookies and cream, strawberry swirls,' Naomie and Layla chanted, taking the assorted tubs of ice cream out of the big freezer.

I arranged seven striped bowls with a spoon in each along our breakfast bar. Then there was a busy time of passing and squeezing and scooping and sprinkling. Before long, we'd finished our ice-cream creations.

Charligh inspected the colourful row of ice-cream sundaes with a satisfied smile. 'Now that's done, we can play the naming game,' she said.

'Which is . . .?' said Allie.

I grabbed one of the bowls overflowing with chocolate fudge ice cream, white chocolate buttons and a dark chocolate syrup and held it up like Mãe did at New Year when doing a champagne toast. 'Choco-loco Bombtastic!' I cried.

Allie's eye sparkled with understanding. She pulled a bowl towards her. 'Silly Lilly Strawberry Sprinkles?'

Naomie gave her the thumbs up, then pointed at one that was adorned with dolly mixture sweets, coloured sprinkles and bright pink syrup. 'Rainbow Ice Explosion!'

We spent the next few minutes coming up with the most inventive names, each one getting more and more silly. In the end we were laughing so hard we only had enough breath to gasp out the names.

Dad had said we could have our ice creams after dinner, which was going to be Dad's Best in the Entire Universe Pizzas. So, after we'd finished the ice-cream naming ceremony, we carefully placed our creations in the freezer and I put *Hairspray* on to watch while we waited for dinner.

Soon Dad poked his head round the corner and whispered so he wouldn't disturb the song 'Good Morning Baltimore', which Charligh was singing along to and perfectly mimicking all the actors' voices. 'What would you all like on the pizzas?' he asked.

I chose varieties I knew none of the girls had ever tried. 'Two Rooster Royales and one Seafood Supreme and one Very Veggie, please,' I said.

I paused the film halfway through when Dad came back in with the pizzas. He brought them on four long wooden trays, two at a time, and placed them on the table. The smell of chicken, caramelized onions, tuna, spicy tomatoes and roasted olives coming from the large slices made my mouth water. We gathered round the table eagerly. Talia's stiffness had worn off a bit. She grabbed a slice of Rooster Royale and shoved it in her mouth.

'*Mmmm!* But it's ho'! Fan-coo, Mha Cam'l,' she said after a few seconds of chewing the hot pizza.

'I'm guessing that means "Thank you, Mr Campbell" – and you're definitely welcome,' Dad said.

Rooster Royale and Seafood Supreme were a hit with everyone. Dad came in a while later to collect the trays and pretended to be horrified that we hadn't left so much as a crumb for him.

We fetched the ice-cream sundaes and ate them while watching the second half of *Hairspray*. Naomie was the worst singer ever. Still, she didn't care one bit that we all laughed until the tears rolled down our cheeks as she warbled along to 'I Know Where I've Been'. She was totally amazing in class and was always getting excellence awards at school, but that evening she was having fun doing the one thing she was completely rubbish at.

Inspired by *Hairspray*, when it ended, we did some karaoke singing, using the games console, and screeched along to all our favourite hits until we went up to my room. Talia had brought a chessboard with all the pieces and spent some time trying to teach us the rules. Allie lost interest and instead was doing handstands, while the rest of us watched Steph try her hardest to beat Talia, who of course won since she was a chess pro. In the final move of their hour-long battle, Talia's queen took Steph's king. Then, finally, it really was time to get ready for bed.

It was almost midnight by the time Dad managed to get us all into my room. I was the last one to fall asleep and my eyes were just shutting as Dad came in to make sure we had all gone to bed.

'Goodnight, princess.' He leaned down to give me a kiss.

I smiled, feeling warm inside my sleeping bag. Dad was here; he wasn't going anywhere. I had the most awesome friends ever. Now all I needed was Mãe to come back where she belonged. Where we all needed her to be.

My shoulders began to tense and the tight feeling in my chest returned as Dad closed the door firmly behind him. I loosened the zip on my sleeping bag and sat up in the darkness, gulping for air. But then I imagined myself dribbling down the wing, making space to shoot and slamming the ball into the goal to win the trophy. Me, becoming a champ just like Rachel Yankey, proving everyone wrong, and making Dad happy and Mãe proud of me. Their own daughter, Jaz Santos-Campbell, star striker!

The tightness in my chest lifted a little. I lay back down and curled up deep into my sleeping bag, giving in to the heavy sleep that was creeping slowly over me like a soft shell.

11

Cakes and Cartwheels

I woke up to Naomie's giggling as she thumbed her way through one of my old joke books. She flicked her hair out of the way. The beads at the bottom of her braids swung like tiny pendulums. She was sitting on my purple sofa bed next to Steph, Layla and Allie.

'Listen up!' Naomie chirped. '"What do you call cheese that's not yours?"'

'I don't know,' said Allie in a monotone.

'"Naa-cho-cheese!"' She exploded into another uncontrollable bout of giggles.

Allie covered her ears. 'It is way too early for that laugh.'

'And it's always too early for your megaphone voice,' Naomie retorted.

Everyone was awake by now and Layla was looking alarmed at the row she had landed in the middle of, while Allie was just glowering even more than usual and clenching and unclenching her fists. I could just picture it now: an angry Allie, an upset Layla and an offended Naomie all kicking a ball around at each other – what could go wrong, right?

'Mmm, can you smell that?' I said quickly. 'Dad's cooking! We'll need lots of that to keep us going during our game later.'

'A game?' said Layla.

I nodded. 'Yup, football. This is a football party. Remember, guys?'

Charligh gave me a sympathetic look but five sleepy faces looked back blankly at me.

'There'll be a box of Candace's cupcakes for the winners,' I added. Dad had bought the cakes from the amazing new bakery on the High Street.

Charligh squealed. 'Let's get ready, quick! I've heard Candace's cupcakes are lush. Who wants to be in my team?'

Layla and Naomie's hands shot up and Charligh said, 'You two are in, then!'

'And Steph, Talia and Allie, you be in mine. Jordan can join your team, Charligh,' I said.

My six friends spent the next thirty minutes scuttling back and forth between the bathroom and my bedroom, getting ready. Finally, as the clock struck nine, we were ready to go down for our pre-game breakfast.

There were plates of warm toast, turkey bacon and scrambled egg spread over the table. Jordan had made Alien Smoothies, a yummy green-coloured concoction of bananas, blueberries and spinach.

'Hungry?' said Jordan as we crammed our plates high with toast and egg.

'Ravenous,' said Charligh. 'We had a busy night –'

'Of non-stop talking, yeah,' Jordan quipped.

Charligh giggled in a silly, high-pitched kind of way that didn't sound at all like her normal laugh. *Ugh.*

Jordan grinned. He liked anyone who laughed at his corny jokes.

After we'd gobbled down our breakfasts, Dad said we should sit for a little while to give our bodies time to digest everything. Eventually we set off to the common together, accompanied by Dad and Jordan carrying the ball and cones. I had stuffed Kinsley into my bag. Maybe she could be our lucky mascot now that she didn't go along to support the Bramrock Rangers any more.

Jordan and Dad sat down at the side to watch while I led my friends in a warm-up. We remembered to stretch our triceps, biceps and hamstrings just like I'd learned to do for dance. It was just as important to make sure we didn't pull any muscles playing football.

'So . . .' Talia said, looking at me with a stern look.

'So what?' I said.

'The rules! Tell them the rules . . . Let's start with the offside rule.'

You've probably already noticed that Talia had A Thing with rules. Although this time she did have a point. Football rules were important.

'I'll start with the basics,' I said, 'since this is just a friendly. Everyone except the goalkeeper can use most parts of their bodies but not their arms or hands. However, the goalkeeper is only allowed to use their hands within the goal box. If you handle the ball outside the lines, the other team gets a throw-in.'

'We use hands for the throw-in,' Talia added.

I nodded. 'So we can't use our hands, but we can use our knees, chests and feet,' I continued, hoping I hadn't missed anything obvious. Most of the girls hadn't played football before, although Allie played netball, and Layla had played hockey in her old school.

Talia jumped in again. 'If you break the rules, including fouling another player, you will get a yellow card or maybe even a red card. Even if you do get a yellow card, you do it again and you'll get a red card.'

'This is a friendly,' I reminded them. A red card meant you'd get sent off, and I didn't want that to happen. 'We aren't giving out red cards today.'

Talia looked terribly crushed.

'I'll be in goal on this side, and Jordan will be in goal for the other. Dad is the ref. Then we'll swap sides after ten minutes,' I reminded them.

The game started. A minute into it and Layla appeared to have forgotten whose team she was on and passed the ball to Allie. Then later, Jordan was so confused he didn't react fast enough when Naomie blasted the ball into her own goal that Jordan was defending. This was the only goal that was scored in the first half. Everyone seemed to completely miss the aim of the game, which was to score points by kicking the ball into the opposition's goal, and seemed to spend most of their time passing to each other or blasting the ball in any direction they could.

'Classic nutmeg,' Talia whooped after Layla kicked the ball through the space between Steph's legs.

'What's that? Did you just call Layla a bad name?' Allie shouted back.

'No, nutmegging is when someone gets the ball through the space in between your legs,' I explained quickly. The last thing I needed was Allie and the others kicking off again.

I glanced at the time as I watched Charligh move with the ball. She was definitely one of the slowest in the game. I wasn't sure if I could last one more minute let alone ten. I signalled to Jordan it was time to swap ends.

He grinned as we walked past each other. 'It could be worse!' he said.

Could it? I wasn't so sure about that. I was frozen stiff after standing around in goal with barely anything to do. I blew on my hands to warm them and hopped from one foot to the other. Things weren't really going exactly the way I'd planned.

But when Dad blew the whistle to signal the end of the game they all cheered enthusiastically. Allie even did a string of perfect cartwheels on the grass in celebration.

What? Just? Happened? Did they just play another match in some parallel universe? Then I smiled. We could work on our skills later, but right now it was all about having fun and showing my friends they could kick a ball.

It was lunchtime by the time we got back. Dad sorted out some sandwiches, while up in my room everyone got their things ready. Dad said we were all winners today, so everyone was getting one of Candace's vanilla cupcakes.

'So what do you think?' I blurted out.

'About?' Naomie asked.

'About having our own football team,' I said.

Steph's eyebrows shot up.

As I got ready to explain about the flyer I'd seen and the seven-a-side tournament, the whole plan sounded a bit daft. Even to me, and it had been my idea. Why would six girls, none of whom were football-mad like me, agree to be in a team that didn't even exist yet? Layla probably couldn't wait to get home to her fashion mags, Naomie had every minute of her time outside school filled with extra tuition and private study, and Steph was just too sensible. And why would Talia, a stickler for the rules, and Allie who was allergic to rules, want to be in the same team? Charligh had only agreed because she was my BBF, but I'm sure she would rather be singing and acting with the drama group than running round the common after a football.

Embarrassed, I pulled out my phone and showed them the web page about the competition.

'I think – well, um, I thought, we could enter this,' I said.

'"Brighton Girls' Under-elevens Seven-a-Side Football Tournament",' read Naomie. 'Seriously?'

'I thought we could win,' I said, although I had to admit those words sounded ridiculous now. I took my phone back, ready to close the page for good.

'Wait! Let's see it properly.' Steph turned my phone round again and scrolled down the page.

'You do have the craziest ideas, Jaz, but . . .' Naomie narrowed her eyes, reading over Steph's shoulder. 'What makes you think we *can't* win?' she said with a confident smile.

Allie nodded her agreement as Steph passed the phone to her and Layla.

Talia frowned but looked thoughtful.

As I watched the hopeful and excited looks on my friends' faces, I suddenly felt I wasn't alone in my dreams. And, just like that, the spark inside that had gone out started to flicker and glow again.

'You're right. I can see it now: Steph is so fast she'll run rings round defenders. Talia can keep us all on track in training sessions and make sure we're following the rules. Allie, you're fearless and have amazing hand-eye co-ordination, so you would be great in goal. Naomie and Layla, if you tackle the forwards like that in a real game, no one will even get near Allie. And as for Charligh, well, obviously she's going to be our spokesperson.'

No one said anything for a few long, awkward seconds.

Surprisingly, Talia spoke up first: 'Count me in!'

'And me!' said Allie.

'Me too!' said Layla.

'And us!' said Charligh, Steph and Naomie together.

'We'll need a name,' I said, leaning back on my elbows, and, as I looked up at the ceiling, I had an idea. 'How about the Stars?' I said. The others followed my gaze.

'Yes! We can be the Bramrock Stars!' they all cried.

'Bramrock Stars FC it is, then!' I grinned.

Now the room was popping with energy and excitement. Charligh was practising her championship acceptance speech, Layla and Allie were trying out different poses for the newspaper feature we would get if we won, and Steph put herself forward for the role of team secretary. Naomie was already talking about team tactics and strategy. Talia pulled me aside and insisted upon the need for us all to look at the official football rule book. Allie butted in and asked quite seriously if it was possible to tear the rule book up.

Then they voted unanimously for me to be team captain. Imagine me being captain of anything! I was a mixture of emotions – part nervous, part chuffed and extremely excited. I was nervous because we only had eight weeks to prepare for the tournament, so it wasn't going to be easy. But then I thought of Mãe, probably eating Sunday lunch with Aunty Bella just now, instead of being here where she belonged, and it made me determined to do it.

A car outside tooted loudly. 'That'll be my mum,' Layla said. Allie and Layla scrambled to grab their bags. I looked out of the window and waved to Mrs Hussani, who beeped her horn back. Naomie and Steph walked back home together, and Talia got picked up by her older sister who was in college. Mrs Gorley was the last one to arrive. I could hear her out in the hall talking to Dad as Charligh pulled on her coat.

'Thanks for having her, Drew,' I heard Charligh's mum say. 'We had a quiet night back at our house,' she joked.

'Well, I'm glad one of us had a peaceful night,' Dad said, smiling pointedly in our direction.

Mrs Gorley lowered her voice and turned her back to us a little. 'How is she doing? Is she getting used to it?' But just then, Charligh, who had left her hairbrush in my room, burst out into the hall on her way upstairs, cutting their conversation short.

I think we can take a not-so-wild guess that when she said 'she' she meant *me*. How could Mrs Gorley even ask if I was getting used to it? It wasn't like a new haircut or a new pair of shoes. You didn't just *get used* to a big chunk of your family falling away. It was like a massive hole had opened up the day Mãe left, but I was sure she must be missing us dreadfully already and would be back any day.

Because mums always do come back, don't they?

12

One More for the Team

Miss Williams was looking at something on her tablet. The wall behind her was filled with canvas paintings she had done of the beautiful scenery on St Kitts. A few weeks ago, on the first day of term when we'd had a 'get to know you' session, she'd told us about her holiday there visiting her grandparents' home over the summer.

'Jaz! To what do I owe this pleasure?' I'd gone to see her just at the start of lunch break. Miss Williams used to fill in for the other teachers when they were off or doing their planning days, but this year she was our main class teacher. She had a kind face and dressed in colourful, floaty skirts and chunky jewellery. Miss Williams told us that we could go to her if we had any problems – and not just to do with English or maths, but even if we were bothered about anything or had trouble with someone else in the class.

'I wondered if you could, like – can you, erm – would you be our supervisor? Kind of like our ... football manager?' I eventually blurted out. 'It's OK if you don't know anything about football. We just need an adult to supervise our training sessions and take us to the tournament. It's a new team – Bramrock Stars. An all-girl football team. I set it up myself, except we're hardly ready yet at all. For the tournament, I mean ...' I babbled on like a runaway train until I ran out of steam and chugged to an awkward stop, hoping I hadn't gone totally off the rails.

Miss Williams held up her hands. 'OK, OK, Jaz,' she said. 'You've drenched me in words. Any more and I'd be drowning in them.'

'That's OK, miss,' I said, backing off.

'Wait, Jaz – No! I mean I'd *love* to be part of this. I don't know much about football, but I did play hockey at school, if that helps?'

Without even thinking, I reached over and gave her a big hug.

'I'll discuss this with Mrs Rivers before I say yes definitely, but I'm sure it will be fine. So . . . you like football, then?'

'I LOVE football! And I'd love it even more if I could play it with the girls,' I said.

I nearly danced my way across the hall until I reached our broken half-table, where all the team were sitting. I paused deliberately. 'So how's lunch today?'

'Hey! Tell us what she said!' demanded Charligh.

'Fine. Since you forced it out of me.' I paused again for dramatic effect, until Allie elbowed me quite sharply in my side.

'Ow! OK . . . well . . . Miss Williams has agreed to supervise our training sessions. So, if you guys are still up for it, we're going to the Brighton seven-a-side tournament!'

Everyone cheered.

*

Later that afternoon, Miss Williams dismissed the rest of the class at home-time but asked me and the others to stay behind. Rosie, Erica and Summer deliberately dawdled in the doorway, shamelessly displaying their nosiness. That is, until Charligh glided over to the door and closed it right in their faces.

My stomach fluttered. What if Miss Williams had changed her mind? What if Mrs Rivers didn't want her to help us?

'Don't look so worried,' said Miss Williams. 'Mrs Rivers said she's excited about your team representing the school and I've completed the online registration form for Bramrock Stars on the website. That's the good news.'

She paused as everyone whooped excitedly.

'What's the bad news, miss?' asked Talia over the noise.

'Unfortunately, the school hasn't got the funds to buy you a new football strip. The boys got there first and the budget for sports equipment has been used up by them. I've asked Mr Roundtree to give us the old shirts, though. Let's see if we can do anything with those – they'll have to do for now.'

Was that all? Just a few days ago, we didn't know if we had a team or not. Now all we had to worry about was our football tops and shorts. I couldn't wait to share the good news with Allie and Layla. We were already halfway to victory and, even if we didn't have a proper strip, we had a manager and – most importantly – a team.

When I got home, I tried to video-chat with Mãe three times, but she never picked up. I frowned. Mãe had barely called since she left. It was getting so hard to speak to her. Had she forgotten about us already?

I slumped back in my bed, feeling defeated for a moment. What I had to say felt too long and important for a text. Then I sat back up and typed out an email on my tablet.

Hi Mãe,

I'm sorry I'm not going to be in the dance showcase. It's rotten luck and it's all thanks to Rosie. But guess what? I'm going to be part of something even better! A girls' seven-a-side football tournament! Me, Charligh,

Naomie, Steph and some other girls are going to be a real team. We're called Bramrock Stars FC. You and Dad can come and watch, and you can cheer us on if we get to the finals. Make that WHEN we get to the finals. Positive thinking – isn't that what you always tell me?

Anyway, just wanted to let you know. Sorry I didn't come with Jordan the other weekend.

Miss you loads,
Jaz xxx

13

Aunty Bella's

I stared out of the car window. Jordan never put up much of a fight about going to see Mãe. In fact, my brother didn't put up any kind of fight. That was just like Jordan, though – he always seemed to be at peace with whatever was going on. As for me, on the other hand, well, it seemed as if I was fighting a never-ending battle. Like now, sitting in Dad's car, which was speeding over the bridge to Brighton.

It wasn't right. Mums weren't meant to be visited. They were meant to be, you know, *there*.

'Dad?'

'Yes, sweetie?'

'Are Aunty Bella's weird hippy friends going to be there?'

'I don't expect so. And, by the way, her friends aren't "weird", they're just . . . alternative.'

'"Alternative" . . .? Huh, that's a grown-up's word for "weird",' I said, pressing my nose against the rain-streaked window. Dad laughed.

My head was hot and achey, and the cool glass soothed the heavy pain behind my eyes. We drove through the automatic gates, which led us into a modern apartment complex. 'You never seemed to mind going before, Miss Grumpy,' said Dad. 'I thought you loved visiting Tia and meeting her friends.'

But before they were only Aunty Bella's friends. Before, they weren't people who probably saw my mum more than I did. Before, Aunty Bella wasn't the one creating a different world for my mother, a world that was taking her away from us.

It was all so different now and I didn't like it. Not one bit.

Jordan had travelled to Winchester with the youth orchestra for a music retreat, so Dad would be at home all by himself. I felt a pang of guilt as we entered the glass lift in Aunty Bella's block of flats.

Aunty Bella swung her front door open. 'Hi! How's my favourite niece?' she exclaimed.

Mãe appeared behind her. 'Oh, Jaz!' she said, wrapping me in a long hug.

'Hi, Tia. Hi, Mãe,' I mumbled. My arms hung awkwardly, lifeless down at my sides. I couldn't explain how, but Mãe felt different.

There was a hard silence. My parents looked at one another. Aunty Bella coughed and gave Mãe a meaningful look, as if reminding her about something.

Mãe blinked. 'Thanks for dropping Jaz off,' she said stiffly. 'I got your text earlier, but you don't need to worry about picking her up for school tomorrow. I can manage.'

Dad looked unsure. 'OK . . . as long as you're certain. I don't mind . . .'

'I'm sure,' she said. Mãe's tone was a little sharper this time.

The atmosphere was thick and bitter, like cream gone sour. Aunty Bella held the door open a bit wider.

Dad smiled tightly. 'Have all the fun, princess,' he said, and turned to go.

I nodded, not quite trusting myself to say the right thing. My stomach flip-flopped and wobbled inside like Granny Campbell's raspberry jelly.

'I thought he'd never leave,' Aunty Bella muttered as the echo of Dad's footsteps faded down the corridor. The ache in my head had become even worse and my mind felt it was being split in two. One half wanted to run after Dad; the other half wanted to stay with Mãe because I'd missed her so much.

I kicked off my shoes and curled up on the sofa in the living room. Everything looked so different from the last time we'd been here.

'Do you like what we've done to the flat?' Mãe asked. 'We decided to jazz it up a little. We've gone for the boho-chic look.'

I nodded, as if I knew that was the name for the vibrant coloured throws that were draped over the sofas and chairs, the plump cushions with gold tassels dotted around, and the bold patterned rugs covering the wooden floors. Aunty Bella was wearing one of Mãe's floral-patterned kaftans. It was full length on Mãe, nearly touching the ground, but on Tia it only went to just below her knees. Dad used to joke that Mãe's little sister had stolen all the height from her. I suppose I took after Mãe, because I was the second shortest girl in the class.

'It was a group effort,' said Aunty Bella. 'Eduardo, Jenny, Roy and Simon – they all chipped in. We wanted to make your mother feel at home here.' She opened her biscuit tin and held it out to me.

It's not her home, though! I wanted to tell her. I wanted to shout it. *She already has a home, with her own nice big room that she shares with Dad and another room where she makes her beautiful designs!* Instead, I fished out a chunky oat-and-raisin cookie. My favourite. But today it stuck in my throat like sawdust. My eyes watered as I began to cough.

Mãe was over in a flash, patting me on the back, and Aunty Bella grabbed a glass of water, which she held at my mouth.

I squeezed my eyes shut for a few seconds and tried to steady myself while my breathing returned to normal. 'You mustn't eat so fast, love,' Aunty Bella said, making room for Mãe to squeeze in next to me. I felt snug and safe under her arm, and much better already. I took small sips of water.

'How's Fussy Forrest, then?' Mãe asked when my cough had subsided.

I grinned. She was probably the only parent at Bramrock Primary who knew and used all my nicknames for the teachers.

I straightened, getting ready to tell her the latest on Fussy, when Aunty Bella piped up: 'Don't worry. I used to hate school, and all my teachers too, and I did all right.' She winked. Aunty Bella did have a cool job: she was a publicist for a publishing company in Brighton. The best way I can think to describe her job is that she's someone who spreads the news about books. She read oodles of stuff by writers from all over the world and thought of great ways to make their work famous. The problem was, I think the story bug had rubbed off on her, because everything you said ended up being a way for her to tell *her* story, usually about things that had happened before I was born.

'I quite like school,' I said.

I noticed a pile of fabric in the corner – sapphire-blue taffeta. A half-unrolled measuring tape and scissors lay on top of it. Tia followed my gaze. 'Isn't the colour simply gorgeous? I heard it's for one of your friends at school who's playing the lead part in the dance showcase. I hope she loves it as much as I do!'

'Rosie isn't my friend,' I said. I didn't miss dance, not even when Rosie had flounced over to me and Charligh one lunchtime to tell us Ms Morgan had given her the lead part. Still, twinges of envy and annoyance pricked at me. To think that the Royal Pain would get to wear my mum's designs onstage instead of me. And in front of hundreds of parents and students too. *The colour will even match her blue eyes*, I thought crossly.

'It's such a gorgeous aroma, isn't it?' Mãe was pointing at the row of strongly scented candles on the low windowsill that were filling the flat with the smell of coconut and vanilla. She inhaled deeply. 'It's like my nasal passages have opened up again now that I've finally kicked the habit – no more stress smoking!'

I blinked in surprise. I'd wanted Mãe to give up smoking for ages – so had Dad and Jordan – but, now that she had, I felt all funny inside. Why hadn't she done this before? Maybe she'd still be back living with us if she had. The quivering flames sparked the memory of the fire at our house *that day* and I felt myself freeze.

'How's the football going? The Bramrock Stars, isn't it?' Mãe said, snapping me out of my thoughts. I smiled, the horrid tense feeling melting as I realized she'd remembered our team name.

'Miss Williams has agreed to be our manager. Although, of course, I'll be the team captain,' I announced.

'Wonderful, *anjinha*! I can't wait to see you shine on the pitch. Forget about the *dança* – it's their loss.'

I glowed inside. Perhaps I could do even more than shine on the field. Perhaps we could bring the trophy back. Mãe, Jordan and I used to go to all Dad's home games when he played for Bramrock Rangers in the Sunday league. We'd puff out the frosty air, warm ourselves with hot food and drinks from the burger van and cheer really loud. It seemed like our family had never gone back to normal after Dad's injury. Mãe and Dad had started either arguing or not talking at all. And now they seemed totally broken.

'Would the team captain like her hair styled as a reward for all her hard work? Cornrows?' Aunty Bella asked.

I was still cross that she had Mãe with her and was pretending that this place, her home, was Mãe's too, but I nodded. I loved getting my hair braided.

She popped into her room and came back with a mirror, comb and a spray bottle filled with hair oil. I sat down on a cushion in front of her and slipped my hairband off so my tight brown curls bounced up and round my head. I held the hand mirror she gave me and watched. First she combed all the tangles out after spraying it with hair oil, then she drew neat lines in my scalp. After each line, she made a long and perfect braid that went from the roots of my hair to the very tips, so that it hung down loose just past my neck.

'I miss doing this – I can't do it on my own hair,' she said, gesturing to her own closely cropped Afro. Tia had cut all her hair off a few years ago. Said it made her feel freer.

I knew what she meant. Even though I hadn't cut mine, my hair in cornrows felt short and light. I wouldn't have to worry about my curls falling out of place and into my eyes when running down the pitch or diving in for a tackle.

'Thanks, Tia,' I said, forgiving her for earlier.

'*Ah, linda!* You're beautiful!' Mãe exclaimed. 'Can you do mine now, please, Bella?' She grinned.

'No, I need to make dinner. Bella's hair shop is closing now.'

'How about I make dinner instead?' Mãe teased.

'Oh, no thanks,' said Aunty Bella.

Unlike Mãe, my aunt was an amazing cook. Food was just about the only thing that Aunty Bella and Dad agreed on. They both liked to cook everything from scratch instead of buying it ready made. Last time we all came round, she and Dad had talked a lot about how important it was to buy fair trade stuff at the supermarket.

That evening Aunty Bella cooked my very favourite chicken meal, *muamba de galinha*, a spicy Angolan stew made with chicken, garlic, chilli and onions. It used to make my tongue burn when I was younger, but now I loved the strong, spicy flavours that rushed through when I bit into the chicken. She served it with soft white rice. I ate more and more until I was full, but

I left just enough room for dessert. She'd made a pumpkin cheesecake for afters.

'Mmm ...' I said through a mouthful of crumbly biscuit, pumpkin and lemon cream.

'Marcus showed me this vegan recipe when I spent Thanksgiving with his family in Texas a few years ago.' Aunty Bella turned to Mãe. 'You remember Marcus, don't you, Iris?'

'Of course. Marcus ... the One Who Got Away. How could I ever forget him?' Tia cackled loudly as Mãe made loud swooning noises. 'Never mind *his* heart – it was *my* heart you broke when you dumped him. I was set on being your bridesmaid. Just imagine ...'

'Imagine, imagine, imagine! Imagine if I'd settled down in a semi-detached house with a boring man, two kids and a dog?' Tia pretended to yawn.

She and Mãe burst into peals of laughter and then stopped abruptly, as if they'd suddenly remembered I was there and had heard what she'd said. I stared down at my hands. What could I say? *Sorry if you think Mãe's life is a boring joke. Sorry she now seems to regret her boring life. Sorry that Dad, Jordan and I even exist.*

The food churned uncomfortably together in my stomach.

'We were going to watch a movie,' Aunty Bella said. 'You can choose.'

'I have school tomorrow,' I said, my voice suddenly very small, matching how I felt. I stood up.

Aunty Bella patted the couch next to her. 'Sit down. It's only nine o'clock. And you can take a sick day tomorrow if you want.'

I frowned. 'I can't take a sick day tomorrow because I'm not sick.' I turned to Mãe. 'You promised Dad you'd get me to school.'

'Of course you'll go to school tomorrow,' Mãe said soothingly. 'The bed's all made up for you. I'll sleep on the couch, so you have the room to yourself. 'Make sure you tie your hair with this to keep your braids neat and soft.' Mãe passed me one of her beautiful silk headscarves, which was on the top of one of her neat fabric piles. It was a deep red with a swirly gold pattern. She gave me a quick hug.

'Night, Mãe. Night, Tia,' I mumbled as I headed off to get ready for bed.

'One more thing', said Aunty Bella unexpectedly. 'What about a football coach?'

'Yes, you must have a coach,' Mãe said, joining in.

'Of course,' I bluffed. I didn't want to tell them that I was planning to be the coach. 'We're still deciding.'

My head spun as I lay in bed. There was so much to get used to. It was just so weird, Mãe living here with Tia. And what they said about a coach. A coach from where? They weren't just handing those out in the middle of town, were they?

There was only one person I could think of who was up to the job, but I didn't know if they would agree to do it. 'Well, there's only one way to find out, right?' I whispered to myself, frowning into the darkness.

14

Training

Mr Roundtree glared at us. We'd trudged our way over to him during afternoon break. The rumour (which I may or may not have started) in our school was that he was really a government spy. Our school caretaker was incredibly talented at becoming invisible when someone needed his help. Except for coaching the boys' football team, the only time Rotten Roundtree *did* appear was when he smelled trouble. He had slunk out from the side of his annexe as soon as we approached it.

'Did I give you a fright?' he asked. 'Were you in the middle of plotting some unmentionable mischief?' He sniffed crossly at Charligh and me, before wiping his nose with the back of his hand.

'No, sir. We want you to coach our football team,' I said.

'What are you on about? I'm already coaching the team and you, my girl, are not on it. Girls and boys have to play separately from Year Five upwards, which is why you weren't allowed to play for the school team last year. You know that.'

'We've made our own team. Me, Charligh and some other girls. There's an all-girls' seven-a-side tournament and we're going to enter.'

'Are you indeed! Well, good luck! I'm sure you'll all need it. Although I suppose you – Santos – aren't so bad . . . for a girl.' He flicked bits of dirt out from under his nails. 'I don't have time. I'm too busy with the real school team – Bramrock Rovers. I've visions of us bringing back the cup, like we did fifteen years ago . . .' His eyes got all misty as he stared back into the distant past.

Charligh and I left Rotten Roundtree to soak in his football fantasies. *Ugh.* He could drown in them for all I cared.

'What do we do now?' Charligh asked.

'I'll be the coach,' I said.

'You?' Charligh looked doubtful.

'Yes, me,' I said with a firm nod of my head. 'Just wait and see!'

I placed the football how-to book I'd got out of the library on my desk and opened my notepad. My mind went blank. I gnawed at my pen. I wrote 'TRAINING' at the top and underlined it with a fluorescent pink pen. Still nothing came to mind. So I underlined it again. Then I stared hard at the football skills book. My mind was still like a heavy ball of nothingness. So I underlined the heading one more time.

I decided it was time to actually open up the book instead of just staring at the cover. I browsed through the chapters, which were called things like 'Basic Skills', 'Warming up' and 'Dribbling', making notes in my pad as I went along.

Before long, the whole pad was filled with scribbles. I had so many ideas about exercises to improve ball control and goal targeting, for defence tackles and, my least favourite shots ever, penalties. Penalty kicks made me nervous and a bit dizzy, just like pirouettes did. Hopefully we wouldn't have to do those, but we had to be prepared.

Dad and I arrived at the common bright and early, but Miss Williams was already there. Then we heard the roar of an engine and Naomie's dad's car came screeching to a halt. Steph, Naomie and Charligh all tumbled out. Mr Osei waved at us from the window, spun his car round and headed away.

Dad chuckled. 'I'm glad you all got here in one piece.'

'Just about,' muttered Naomie. 'Have you seen the way my dad drives?'

As we waited for the others to arrive, Dad and Miss Williams lined up the cones for the ball-control drill. We left a small space between the cones to get everyone used to dribbling in tight spaces. Talia arrived, followed closely by Layla and Allie, who came on their bikes.

First we discussed subs – that was the money we'd pay at every session so we could save up and buy things like new training equipment and fruit and other treats for after our training sessions.

I couldn't wait to get started. The first thing we had to get out of the way was team positions. I decided we'd do a 2-2-2 formation. The goalie goes at the back; then in the next row are two players – the left and right defenders; then the left and right midfielders are in front of them; and, finally, the left and right forwards. It was the simplest way of doing it.

'Naomie, right back. Steph, right mid. Allie in goal. Talia can be right forward –' I carried on, ignoring the scowls on almost everyone's face. 'Charligh, left back and, Layla, you're left mid. I'm left forward.'

'Left back is so hard,' grumbled Charligh. 'Why do I need to be left back? Right wouldn't be so bad, but left . . .'

'Right back is just as bad, but I don't mind swapping with you,' Naomie offered.

'I can't be a forward. It's too much pressure on me to score,' Talia said, folding her arms.

I rolled my eyes. 'Scoring is the whole point of the game, Talia.'

'So what are you saying? The rest of us are pointless, then?' Layla asked.

'No, no, that's not what I mean.' I took a deep breath and started again. 'Two weeks – give it a try for two weeks. We can always change positions after that,' I pleaded.

There was a frosty silence.

'Look, we're wasting time,' Steph said. 'Let's just make the best of our positions. Apart from Talia and Jaz, we've never played much football at all so we can't really say we don't like our positions, can we?'

I smiled at her gratefully. You know how some people are just great at making others see the best in every situation? Well, Steph was one of those people.

Everyone reluctantly agreed to give it a try. We got started with a run round the perimeter of the common.

Our 'gentle' warm-up run ended with Allie running flat into Talia's back, then Layla and Naomie moaning they hadn't signed up to train for a marathon. Charligh kept tripping over her own feet during the ball-control drill. For that, we did a shuttle run, dribbling a special small ball in and out of the cones. I watched helplessly as our first training session fell apart bit by bit till the whole team collapsed into a sullen mob.

I know what you're thinking – it can't get any worse, right? I know, because that's *exactly* what I was thinking too – until Naomie blasted a ball in Charligh's face by accident. Charligh was OK, and would have forgotten all about it if Allie hadn't exploded with laughter, which meant Charligh threw an ultra-dramatic strop that could have won her an Oscar. And, as for Talia, well – she spent so much time shouting random football rules at us that she kept missing the ball.

When Miss Williams blew her whistle for the end of the session, we all marched off in what seemed like seven different directions without much more than a curt goodbye to each other. I seriously wondered if there would ever be another training session.

'Don't worry, it'll be fine,' Dad said, squeezing my shoulder gently as I watched my team splinter off.

But when we got home I ran straight to my room and dragged Kinsley off the top bunk. I buried my face in my stuffed elephant's soft fur.

'Oh, Kinsley,' I said. 'What are we going to do?' I studied her face for an answer and sighed at her closed expression.

I'd obviously have to figure this one out on my own.

15

A New Coach

I slid the book across the library counter to Rhiannon for her to check back in. 'Any good?' she said.

'I did write loads of training schedules with it . . . only . . .' I hesitated. 'I don't know if my team will come back to train again. They were a bit all over the place.'

'Who's the coach?'

'Me,' I said defensively. 'I'm left forward, team captain *and* coach.'

Rhiannon shrugged. 'OK, go on. I'll be the coach.'

I gaped at her. 'Do you even know anything about football?' I asked.

'I know enough,' she said evenly. 'Let's just say football's a big deal in my family. Long story.' She pretended to yawn, as if it would bore me.

'It's seven-a-side,' I said carefully. 'Not like a full team that usually has –'

'Eleven.' Rhiannon rolled her eyes. 'Come on, give me some credit. I think everyone knows *that*.' She tapped her nails on the counter impatiently. 'Do you want my help or not?'

I didn't imagine Rhiannon knew much about football, but it would be rude to turn down her offer, and I could see that for some reason she really wanted to be our coach. So I pasted on my cheeriest smile, the one I gave to Granny Campbell, who lived up in Dundee, when she gave me the lumpy hat she'd knitted to 'keep ma heid warm'.

'Our next training session is tomorrow in the common. We start at 5 p.m. . . . Are you working then?' I asked hopefully.

'You're in luck. I finish at three, so that gives me enough time to go home, grab something to eat and get changed before I meet you guys there.'

I stepped aside then, to let the woman behind me get to the counter.

'See you tomorrow at five,' Rhiannon called after me.

The next day at school, I decided the best way to make sure everyone came to the training session was to tell them I'd a special announcement to make.

'What kind of announcement?' Charligh said.

'A special one,' I had said, wiggling my eyebrows up and down, hoping I looked mysterious enough. No one, not even my BBF, was going to find out about this until they got there. In fact, no one, *especially* my BBF, was going to know, because, let's face it – Charligh sucked at keeping secrets.

Rhiannon arrived at the common at 5 p.m. sharp. Her hair was tied up in a high ponytail and she was wearing charcoal-grey sports leggings and a matching baggy top. I didn't even recognize her at first. Without the make-up, she looked much younger.

My team-mates stared at her.

Rhiannon pulled out two blankets from her huge holdall, and spread them out on the grass.

'Since your team captain has decided not to introduce us – bit rude, Jaz – I'll do the honours. I'm Rhiannon O'Shea.'

'Lovely to have you on board, Rhiannon!' Miss Williams said. 'Your face looks familiar,' she added.

Rhiannon nodded. 'You might have seen me around before. In the library or at the Hungry Readers cafe –'

'Or on Instagram,' Allie broke in.

Layla nudged her.

'What are you on about?' I said.

'She's a big star on Instagram. She's got about twenty thousand followers,' Allie said.

Rhiannon frowned. 'How do you two know – are you even old enough to be on Insta?'

Allie shrugged. 'It's my big sister's account. She showed it to me after she told me she'd seen one of her favourite bloggers at the Hungry Readers cafe. You study make-up artistry at Bramrock College, and you post things about make-up and food . . . and more food. You like your food, don't you?'

I wished I was close enough to elbow Allie to shut her up, but Rhiannon grinned.

'All of that is true: I am a make-up artist in training and, yep, I love my grub. Now, that brings me to the first lesson of today's session. Can everyone sit down on one of the blankets please?'

Everyone except Miss Williams grabbed a spot on a blanket.

'OK. Tell me your name and position.'

Naomie went first, then Charligh, and we kept on going till we'd all spoken.

'So, as I was saying, food is fuel. We need food to give us the energy to run, kick, shoot, save and dribble on the pitch. So make sure you eat a balanced diet. Protein and calcium, which you can get from lean meat, seafood, beans and nuts, help repair and strengthen your bones. Carbs give you energy – you'll find them in foods like pasta, rice and potatoes. And plenty of fruit and veg. They give you all the nutrients – that's vitamins and minerals – that your body needs to work properly and fight infections and heal itself from sickness. And not just before training, but all the time. That's what proper footballers do.'

Then Rhiannon asked us all to think hard about what we thought the main purpose of our position was. She had come prepared with a notepad. She jotted down the best ideas for what each position was responsible for and said she would give us all a copy at the end. After that, she asked us what we would like to concentrate on the most. Some said dribbling, others said defending or shooting. Eventually she asked each one of us to come prepared to lead an exercise over the next few weeks.

'Isn't that your job?' Charligh asked.

'I'm the official coach, so I tie everything together, but the best way for this to work is for everyone to get involved. Whether coach or player – or supervisor,' she said with a nod to Miss Williams, 'we all have something to offer. Agreed?'

'Agreed!' everyone yelled. I couldn't believe how enthusiastic the team was and we hadn't even played any football yet.

'I don't think my football skills are quite up to scratch, but I'm happy to follow your lead!' Miss Williams said with a warm smile.

Rhiannon wrote a list of everything we needed

to bring next time to keep us safe and help us play our best football:

Shin guards
Bottle of water
Football boots
Trainers
Tracksuit or shorts
Our whole selves!

Talia frowned. 'What does the last one mean?'

Rhiannon smiled. 'It means you all have your own special strengths and skills. It's all right to be inspired by others – but always be you!'

While we'd been talking, Miss Williams had set up the cones and the goals and was now handing out the neon-yellow bibs. Rhiannon let me lead the warm-up. She said that next time she'd pick someone else to do it so we'd all get a fair turn. Then we moved on to some basic passing exercises. Miss Williams even got involved, so we had four pairs of players passing to each other. It was short, firm shoves across to our partner and then they passed back to us.

We changed partners for this every couple of minutes.

After that, Rhiannon asked me to demonstrate some dribbling – what Allie called my fancy footwork. When we'd done dance, I'd felt like an awkward giraffe, but now the footwork and form I'd learned from Ms Morgan seemed to help me dribble really fast. We ended with a game of Silent Dance Statues, where we had to follow Rhiannon's moves, then freeze the minute she did.

'That game was fun,' puffed Layla, 'but what was the point?'

'This time I'll give you the answer,' said Rhiannon, 'but next time I show you a game I want everyone to think hard for yourselves about what its purpose is. Silent Dance Statues is a way of practising mirroring and reacting quickly to other people's movement.'

Everyone left the session looking a lot happier than last time.

'Thanks, Rhi,' I said gratefully as she helped me pack up the cones. 'Training definitely went better with you as our coach!'

We were lucky to have Rhiannon. I didn't

know if it was enough to get our team ready in time, but it was definitely a start. My team-mates didn't know it, but this was the beginning of a real chance to get my mum home.

16

A Friendly

I'd always thought I was a bit lazy and easily distracted; a lot of my teachers said so anyway, especially Fussy Forrest. But over the next few weeks, I made sure we trained every chance we could get on the common. Rhiannon got her staff rota at the library three weeks in advance. She had asked her manager, Molly, to make sure she was on an early shift during the week so we could meet in the evenings, and on the late shift on Saturday so we could train early in the morning.

Rhiannon had organized a friendly with the women's team from Brighton University on Sunday afternoon. It was our first game and, even though we weren't going to play as a team, we were excited to be mixed in with the uni students. There were about thirteen of them, with different levels of football skills.

'The idea is you'll learn from them and they'll learn from you,' Rhiannon said.

'You think they want to learn from us?' Allie said doubtfully. 'Adults never listen to kids where I'm from.'

'Well, they do here,' Rhiannon said firmly.

So, on Sunday we all went prepared. By now, everyone had the proper gear: shin guards, football shoes and goalie gloves for Allie. We were playing at the sports centre in Bramrock, next to the university accommodation where a lot of the students lived. It was a brightly lit gated pitch next to several other pitches that all had games going on in them. The best thing was that both Mãe and Dad were here to watch. I knew Dad wouldn't have missed it for the world, but Mãe had surprised me by calling to say she was going to drop by. Even more surprising, she'd arrived early and was now standing next to Dad. Mrs Gorley, Mrs Hussani and Mr Osei were there too.

I smiled. Last time my parents had been out anywhere together except for doing the weekly grocery shop was when Fussy Forrest had called them in to be moaned at about the state of my handwriting or something daft like that. It was good to see them together now not being angry or having to discuss my 'behaviour'.

Rhiannon gave me a blue bib. Team Blue was playing Team Yellow, which was Allie, Steph and three university students. I was the only one from Bramrock Stars FC in Team Yellow. I could tell my older team-mates had all been playing for a while. They were good, really good. I was one of the shortest players in Bramrock Stars so I felt extra tiny here.

I think the rest of Team Blue reckoned I wouldn't be any good, as for the first five minutes none of them passed to me. Eventually a tall, strong-looking girl called Lucy booted the ball to me, as Steph and one of the student players from Team Yellow thundered her way. At last, I was off! *Right foot, left foot, right foot* – I stopped suddenly and pulled my right leg over the ball as if I was going to kick it forward. Instead, I flicked it over to the side before charging into the open space and collecting the ball again. I glanced over and saw Dad and Mãe deep in conversation. I frowned, almost tempted to shout to get their attention. Just then, a student player from the Yellows came barrelling into me, stealing the ball away before blasting it up to our goal.

'Ouf!' I yelled as I was shoved to the ground, winded.

'Less showing off, Twinkle Toes, and more of the scoring.' Lucy yanked me up before shooting off to help the defence.

I followed her on the other side, staying close to the defender who had got possession off me earlier. Our goalie blocked three hard attempts at the goal and after the third time she kicked the ball out far and wide. I took the opportunity to break free from the player who was marking me and chased the ball. This time I wasn't going to lose it. I sneaked a look to the side: Mãe and Dad still weren't watching and now Mãe's head was bobbing the way it did when she was cross.

I turned back to the ball, remembering where I was, and gave it my best shot, as Allie came thundering out for a sliding tackle. The ball sailed into the top right-hand corner of the goal ... before bouncing off the corner into Allie's gloved hands. Good save by Allie. Bad shot by me.

I dusted myself off as Rhiannon blew the whistle for the end of the game. There would be a five-minute break before a Reds against Greens game. While the other players milled around the coaches who were giving out refreshments, I jogged over to the huddle of parents. Dad was rubbing his head and looking glum.

'Dad,' I said, 'where's Mãe?'

'Your mum had to take off. She sends her love and says she's sorry she couldn't stay.' Dad stooped down and gave me a warm hug. 'She'll make it up to you. Great game by the way, Jaz super striker!'

Super striker? *Yeah, right! I didn't even score any goals*, I thought, feeling cross with myself. I couldn't help but wonder whether Dad and Mãe would maybe have paid more attention if I had.

I wandered back over to watch the next game. Rhiannon sat next to me as the uni coach was refereeing now.

'Bad luck about that last shot,' she said. 'You did everything right – your goal was just half an inch wide of the bar.'

I mumbled a thank you, still staring back at Dad, who looked a million miles away. Rhiannon and Dad were just being nice, but I knew I'd let everyone down. I could have played so much better. Maybe that's why Mãe had left early. She had probably expected me to play like a pro and not mess things up. No wonder she hadn't even bothered to stay till the end. I bit my lip.

Next time, I'd have to make sure there were no mistakes.

Football Heroes

Rhiannon had given us a homework task to complete. We each had to research a football player and say what we admired about them. So, after forty-five minutes' practising heading the ball, shuttle dribbling and one-touch passing, we all gathered round to give our short presentations.

Allie started off. 'Mine is David Seaman. He was the goalie for Arsenal back in the nineties and had seventy-five caps for England. They say he had safe hands. That's his superpower.'

'Good choice,' said Rhiannon. 'Safe hands – isn't that what every goalkeeper wants? A great goalie from the Women's Super League is Becky Spencer who plays for Spurs – look up some videos of her saves.'

Steph went next. 'Mine is Raheem Sterling. He does a lot of charity work and stands up for what he believes in.'

'Steph makes a good point here,' said Rhiannon. 'You don't need to pick your favourite player just by what they do *on* the pitch. What they do *off* the pitch can matter just as much. That's why some players become role models.' She nodded to Layla to go next.

'Megan Rapinoe. She's a player from the US. I like her because she's an unpredictable player. No one know what she'll do next, so she takes her opponents by surprise.' Layla grinned. 'And sometimes she has pink hair.'

Charligh chose Alex Scott, the former Arsenal defender who used to play for England. She said if the theatre didn't work out, she'd love to become a football presenter like she was.

We went down the line, everyone saying who they'd chosen and why, until it was just me left.

Before I could even open my mouth, everyone chorused, '*Rachel Yankey!*'

'Hey, maybe I was going to choose someone else,' I protested.

'Well, were you?' said Naomie.

'OK, fine!' I laughed. 'I was going to pick Rachel and the reason is she has speed and skill. She played for Arsenal Ladies and I reckon she was the best left forward ever! Plus, she was the most capped player in English football history. She had 129 caps for England. But if I didn't pick her it would probably be Ji So-yun.'

'Great! Well done, girls.' Rhiannon looked very pleased with us all.

'You didn't tell us your favourite player, Rhi,' said Allie.

Rhiannon grinned. 'OK, but I can't choose just one so I'll name three! First Marta, of course – she's to women's football what Pelé is to the men's game! Also Jenni Hermoso and Vivianne Miedema. I could go on, but there are just so many brilliant women players! I know some of you know more about players than others, but it's important for all of you to think about what makes our favourite players so great. Maybe we can aim to work on that one thing and integrate it into our game.' We all nodded.

Rhiannon looked at her watch. 'Are you all still OK to gather up the cones and bibs and bring them to the library? My shift starts in five minutes and I don't want to be late.' She had already leaped to her feet and begun unlocking her bike from the tree. She gave a cheerful wave as she set off, pedalling hard.

Suddenly, Zach and his rotten crew appeared.

'Oi, Santos-Campbell – move! The professionals are playing now.' He gave a toothy grin, like he'd said something really clever.

'We're going,' broke in Steph smoothly. 'After we've warmed down, the common's all yours.'

Zach didn't even look at Steph. His eyes were fixed on me and he continued as if she hadn't spoken. 'I said NOW!'

I felt the heat rising in my face and was about to say something when Layla stepped forward. 'We aren't going anywhere,' she said.

'Can you hear that mouse?' Sebastian said.

Allie and I moved up to stand on either side of Layla. I folded my arms.

'All join in . . . the girls are in the BIN! All join in, the girls are in the BIN!' Zach's friends chorused behind him.

Bully Boy Bacon dug into his grimy pockets and came out with a handful of orange peel and sweet wrappers. 'Here, have this. Rubbish should be with other rubbish,' and he chucked it all over the three of us.

Allie's face went bright red with anger and she lunged towards Zach, who stepped back, laughing.

Layla put her hand on Allie's shoulder. 'They're just trying to get us into trouble. Don't let them get to you,' she pleaded, her eyes filling with tears.

The other Year 6 girls and I made a shield, standing in front of Allie and Layla. 'All join in, the BOYS are in the bin!' I yelled back, and the others joined in the chant.

It went on like that forever, even when a jogger came along and told us we should be ashamed of ourselves for making that racket – 'Especially the young ladies,' she said disapprovingly. That made us girls even crosser. Why was it any worse for 'young ladies' to be 'making a racket' than the boys? It was the boys who'd started it. It just wasn't fair! None of it was.

Layla was hiccupping in between tears, and Steph had to drag Allie away to take deep breaths so she wouldn't pulverize the boys. Still, we stood our ground and eventually the boys moved on to another side of the common because they realized we weren't going to give way.

We helped Steph pick up the rubbish. Even though it was the boys' mess, we couldn't bear to leave all that litter on the ground, and Steph reckoned the orange peel would make wonderful compost for her garden. Doing something public-spirited helped us calm down a bit anyway. Then after we'd warmed down we set off.

'He'll think twice before pushing us around again,' said Naomie as we hurried to the Hungry Readers cafe.

I'd always thought Layla was rather timid, but when she stood up to Zach I saw how brave she really was, and I told her so. She was probably the gentlest of all of us, but she'd been the first one to stand firm with me against the bullying. In fact, we'd all held our ground.

Hmm, I thought, *the Bramrock Stars are tougher than anyone expected!*

18

Mind Your Business

'I was looking over our accounts last night . . . We only have £26.87 left after buying those refreshments for our practice game. And it's not as if we had a lot to begin with,' Steph said, sipping on her hot chocolate at the Hungry Readers cafe. 'And the training equipment, and the indoor hall hire that time the grass was too icy to play outside. We still have to pay for the minibus to take us to the tournament, remember? And that costs a lot. The cheapest one I could find online was £40 an hour, and we would need it for about three hours, so that's £120.'

'What are we going to do?' Talia said, her brows knitting together.

'I have an idea,' said Charligh, lowering her voice. She signalled for us to lean in. 'Maybe we can hitch-hike!' She took a swig of her drink and tried to stifle her laughter, but ended up snorting lemonade through her nose.

Naomie rolled her eyes. 'Classy. Very classy, Gorley.'

'This is definitely not a laughing matter,' I said.

Steph dabbed at the lemonade-splattered table with a paper towel.

'You sound just like Ms Morgan or even worse . . . Wait, you sound like Fussy Forrest!' Charligh complained.

I shrugged. 'Whatever! This is important. No minibus equals no tournament!'

Allie folded her arms. 'It's not fair that we need to pay for the minibus to get there, *and* we've got the oldest, tattiest football strip to wear.'

'I know,' said Naomie. 'The school shouldn't be allowed to spend all the budget on the boys' team. It's like they don't think we're worth it. If they give us a chance, we'll be every bit as good.'

Miss Williams had dug out the old football shirts from years ago for us to use. We were grateful, but they did look so grey and shabby.

'I'll sort those out,' offered Layla. 'I know how to tie-dye fabric – my mum showed me. They won't look anything like the state we got them in after that,' she assured us.

'Good,' Naomie said. 'At least that's one thing sorted, but we still need to raise more money. The minibus hire costs £120, so I've calculated we're £93.13 short.'

'How about a cake sale?' I said.

Charligh crossed her arms and made a face, as if fending off a flying porcupine. 'Will it be you doing the baking? Don't you remember the last cake you made?'

'Can you all stop going on about that?' I said huffily.

'Well, if you think about it, Jaz,' said Layla, 'if you hadn't made your yucky chilli cake, you wouldn't have been dropped from dance, and maybe you wouldn't have started this team. None of us would be here now!'

That's what I loved about Layla. She always looked for the bright side in everything and I suppose, when you looked at it that way, I did have a lot to thank my chilli cake for. Still, it certainly wouldn't have sold very well at a cake sale.

Then a great idea popped into my head. 'Pizza! We can have a pizza sale!' I said. 'I can make the dough and we can all do the toppings.'

Just when I thought my great idea couldn't get any better, Layla chipped in: 'Why don't we do dessert pizza? You know, pizzas with sweet toppings? I had them in Brighton over the summer, but I don't think you can find them in Bramrock. We'd get heaps of customers!'

We took a vote. Every single one of us were in favour of Layla's great(er) idea. A pop-up dessert pizza stall to raise the money we needed for the minibus! The tournament was only two weeks away, so it had to be this Saturday.

'We can have it at my house,' Layla said. 'My mum always says I should invite more friends over.'

Steph typed everything up in her phone notes as we made a 'who's getting what' list. We usually had some ingredients for dough at home, but we would need more than that for the pizza pop-up.

Allie, Layla and I wrote Naomie a list of ingredients for both the dough and the sweet toppings. After working out how many pizzas we'd have to sell at £2 a slice, and thinking about some recipes, Naomie calculated the amounts we needed of each ingredient.

'We always have lots of bananas and strawberries in our house,' Talia added. 'I could bring as much as I can squeeze into my gran's shopping trolley.'

I grinned at the thought of her dragging an old shopping trolley over to Layla's.

'Thanks, Talia.'

'How are we going to publicize it?' Naomie asked.

'What does that mean?' Allie said.

'It means – how do we get the news out?' Steph explained.

'Why didn't you just say that?' Allie said. 'It'll be easy. I'll make some posters and flyers on my sister's iPad.'

When Rhiannon popped over to join us during her tea break, we told her our plan.

'Sounds good,' she said with a grin. 'I'll put up some of the posters here in the library and post it on my Instagram. I have tons of local followers.'

I was beginning to feel more positive about everything. I may have failed at dance, bake-offs and pretty much everything else, but this was my way to prove to everyone I was a star. I could just imagine lifting that trophy. Zach and his mates would be taking back their unkind words and my parents would be so happy. Finally. Dad's eyes would stop being so sad when he smiled, and Mãe would be so proud she would start remembering me more often. And they would be a whole lot nicer to each other. If the Bramrock Stars went all the way to the final and won, it could change everything.

'Yes! Let's do it, Stars!' I said.

19

The Pop-up

'Follow me, girls,' Mrs Hussani said. We followed her through the long, maze-like route from the front door to their huge kitchen, carrying the bags of ingredients we had brought.

Layla greeted us with a wave.

'I was all ready for a dinner party with the ladies from the Neighbourhood Watch committee,' said Mrs Hussani. 'But it appears they all got food poisoning from another party they were at a couple of days ago, so we had to cancel. So, as I was saying, there's plenty of fruit and sweet toppings for you to use.' She pulled open their cavernous fridge.

'Thank you!' Charligh squealed excitedly.

'You're welcome, love. I'll be in the living room while you get the pizzas ready. Layla, make sure you call me when you're ready to put them in the oven so I can supervise. I don't want anyone to burn themselves. And please be very careful with the sharp knives.'

It was an airy open-plan kitchen and lounge, so she'd be able to see us from her armchair.

'*Mu-uum!* We're not babies,' Layla broke in, folding her arms.

'OK, OK,' Mrs Hussani said, retreating to a safe but watchful distance.

Layla stretched out her hands and wiggled her fingers at everyone. Her nails were painted pink with a silver streak along the tips.

'I've just got these done. They're not the best nails for pizza-making, sorry.' She tapped the side of her head as if an idea had just come to her. 'How about you all make and serve the pizza while I handle the money? I don't mind – really I don't. It's teamwork, after all, so we'll all have an important job to do.'

I was pretty sure she had planned this as I knew she wasn't interested in cooking at all, but there was that thing about too many cooks in the kitchen so I was more than happy for her to handle the money.

'Great idea, Layla. Thanks!' I said.

We'd decided the pizza pop-up would open at midday so that people could buy something to have after their lunch. I looked at the recipe for dough that Dad had written out for me; I'd made it so many times. *You could make this with your eyes closed*, Dad had told me at breakfast. I hoped he was right. I bit my lip as the clock struck ten. Our pizza kitchen was two hours away from opening – we had to get started!

'Talia, you're the sprinkler,' I said. I pointed out the colourful jars of blue, pink and silver edible glitter, the white chocolate flakes, the cinnamon and the rainbow sprinkles. 'Make sure every pizza has just the right amount of them.

'Allie, you do the toppings for the Chocolate Strawberry pizza –' I handed her the recipe.

'Steph and Charligh, you can be in charge of the Fruit Burst pizza and the Nutty Banana too.

'Naomie, can you do the Cinnamon Wheel one, please?'

I washed my hands and started preparing the soft dough on the freshly floured work surface. First I sieved the flour on to the worktop and added a pinch of salt. Then I mixed water, a little olive oil and yeast together. Next, making a well in the middle of the flour and salt, I added the wet ingredients and kneaded them in until everything was nice and soft and springy. I knew if I added too much water the dough mixture would come out heavy and sticky, but if I didn't add enough it would be too crumbly and dry. It was a delicate operation that I had to get right.

After forming the dough into a large, flat circle, I passed the first pizza base to the others so they could dress it generously with the toppings – fruit, chocolate (milk, dark and white), cream cheese, nuts or crushed cookies. And then lastly the pizza went to Talia for the finishing touches.

By eleven we had our first batches of pizzas ready to put in the oven. Mrs Hussani slid them on to the oven racks and set the timer for twelve minutes while we moved on to start the next batch. When the timer went off, Mrs Hussani took the pizzas out one by one and set them on cooling racks on the worktops. We worked hard on the second batch, making sure they looked as delicious as the first. This time, Mrs Hussani let us put them carefully into the oven ourselves using her thick oven gloves.

By noon, we were all ready with trays of wonderful-smelling slices of pizza. We placed special heatproof coverings over them to stop them getting too cold out in the crisp November air.

'What if no one comes?' said Talia.

'They'll come,' said Allie, banging her hand on the table on each word with such a fierceness that it was lucky it didn't break.

Maybe Allie's banging worked because, twenty minutes later, the Hussanis' front garden was crowded with customers.

'I'm so impressed that you girls cooked all this yourself. This pizza smells better than some of the ones they serve up in the best restaurants in town,' a man said as he handed over a crisp £5 note in exchange for two slices of pizza. 'Keep the change – you deserve it,' he added.

Layla grinned as she put the coins back into the money box.

The stream of lunchtime customers finally died down just after three! Steph, Talia and I spent the next couple of hours making more pizzas while the others tidied up in the front garden.

At around five o'clock, the crowd surged again, with more people than ever.

'Oh no, it's the VIPs!' Charligh said. Rosie, Summer and Erica rolled up on their scooters and I gave them what I hoped was my Very Irritating People are Bad for Business look. To my surprise, each of them bought a slice of the Fruit Burst pizza.

Then Rosie smiled her usual syrupy smile – you know, the kind she always gave you right before she said something nasty. 'I do hope you get to the tournament,' she said very politely. She smiled again – *that* smile. 'It will give us the biggest laugh of the year. You were hopeless at dance and there's no way *you* can lead this team of losers to win anything.'

I stepped forward, glowering, but Steph laid a calming hand on my shoulder. 'Don't. They're not worth it,' she said.

'Exactly!' Allie was nodding vigorously. She pounded her fist into the palm of her hand, which made Erica jump a mile. 'We're going to SMASH it on the pitch!' said Allie loudly.

The VIPs retreated fast as Allie continued to scowl at them, until she was distracted by a big family who came up to the table with a long order. I waved Rosie and her gang off as they sped away on their scooters. If that awful chilli-cake fiasco had taught me anything, it was that allowing myself to be provoked by Rosie's smugness wasn't a good idea.

We sold our last pizza to an elderly woman with a small white poodle, which yapped happily as it trotted away beside her on its lead.

Finally, Bramrock's first dessert pizza pop-up was closed and it was time to clear up and count our takings for the day. With the money we already had and a promise of an extra £5 from Dad if we worked hard today, we'd worked out that we needed nearly £90 more to hire the minibus.

We gathered round the huge dining table while Steph counted the takings and wrote the total down. We held our breath as Naomie did the second count to make sure the figures were right.

She put down the last coin. 'So,' she said, 'we didn't make our target profit amount of £90.'

I blew out heavily in disappointment.

Naomie exchanged a secret smile with Steph.

'We made £112.60 to be exact,' finished Naomie.

'Enough for the minibus and then some!' Steph said, piling all the notes and coins into the red money box as the rest of us whooped and clapped.

I tingled all over with excitement. We were one step closer to achieving my dream.

Bramrock Stars were going to the tournament!

20

Tournament Day

Today was the day.

We had to win all three of our games. *There's no room for silly mistakes*, I thought with a sinking feeling deep in my belly.

By 8 a.m., a blue minibus was waiting in the library car park to pick us up. Miss Williams and Rhiannon were travelling with us, and so was Dad, Jordan, Allie's mum and Talia's gran. Mãe was driving down with Aunty Bella.

'The day we've been training so hard for has arrived! I've been waiting my whole life for this moment,' Charligh gasped dramatically, recording herself on her phone camera.

'But you only started playing earlier this term,' Talia said.

'*Tomayto, tomahto*,' muttered Charligh in her New York accent. She frowned at Talia, then twisted a little to make sure Talia wasn't in the background to interrupt her next video attempt.

'What if we get stage fright?' Layla asked.

'Stage fright? On the football pitch? Is that even a thing?' Allie scoffed. She had nerves of steel.

'We won't,' Steph said firmly, 'and it's not like there's just one of us, Layla. We have each other, don't we?' She looked round at everyone.

We all nodded in agreement.

The minibus turned into the community sports park in Hove. We went past a pond with lightly frosted lilies resting on the surface. The sun's rays danced over the shimmering silver pool like a dainty ballerina as we drove round it. I pulled Kinsley out of my bag and hugged her tight.

We reached a large tarmac car park. There were rows and rows of coaches already parked there dwarfing our tiny vehicle. For the first time that day, everyone was quiet as we watched troops of girls spilling out of the giant coaches.

My stomach did loops, knots and bows in a dozen places as we headed over to the registration desk to sign up and receive our tournament information packs. Dad went off with Jordan and the other parents to find Mãe and Aunty Bella while we followed the signs to the changing rooms with Miss Williams.

When we got there, the first thing we did was study the sheet headed GROUP FIXTURE TIMETABLE, which was stuck on the inside of the door.

'Group B,' Steph read out. 'We're playing Windmill Villa, Brighton Dynamos and the Hove Cosmos.'

I'd never heard of Windmill Villa or Brighton Dynamos before, which meant they were probably new on the scene like us. The Hove Cosmos, on the other hand, were well known. They'd played together in the Brighton and Hove girls' seven-a-side league for at least two years.

'Their star player is Harriet Goldwater,' I said. 'She's tipped to play for the Brighton County Schools under-thirteens squad,' I said.

I was interrupted by a loud cry from Charligh. We looked over to where she was sitting cross-legged. She had unzipped the holdall containing our football kits

Charligh held one out. It definitely wasn't a drab grey any more. Now it was a sickly riot of pink, brown and green. An explosion of colours had run and seeped into one another.

'This literally looks like the twins have been sick on it,' said Charligh. She held it at arm's length, as if there really was baby vomit smeared on the shirts.

We all turned to Layla, looking aghast.

'What were you thinking?' I groaned. 'You said you were going to customize the shirts . . . and make them look better, not worse!'

'I tie-dyed them,' Layla said, 'like I said I would, but it – but it went a bit wrong.' Her voice was all thin and quivery, and I felt a little sorry for her.

'A bit? How about a lot! It looks like the result of a war in a paint factory,' Talia said.

Layla blushed a deep red and bit her bottom lip.

I stripped down to my vest, pulled on my shorts and threw on one of the shirts. Charligh and

Talia were absolutely right – it looked terrible. I made a mental note never to let Layla loose on our football shirts again. But as for today – we had a game to win. Three games, to be exact.

'Look, who gives a hoot what we look like?' I said. 'We're here to WIN!'

'You look really awful!' Allie crowed.

'Allie,' Talia said, speaking really slowly as if to a very small child, 'what do you think you'll look like? We're all going to be wearing the same.'

Allie looked as miserable as Charligh as it sank in.

'It's not so bad . . .' I began, turning this way and that in the mirror. But I wasn't even kidding myself. It was The Worst.

'It's a disaster,' said Talia flatly. She sat down on the metal bench and tucked her legs under her.

'Well, we need to wear them,' Naomie said with a shrug.

'It's all right for you,' said Allie, her lips curling. 'You look amazing in anything.' She was the only person who could give someone else a compliment with a sour expression on her face.

Naomie slipped one of the shirts on with her shorts and twirled around for us. Then she took a quick selfie with her phone. She giggled as she looked at the picture. 'See, I don't,' she said. 'I look terrible too.'

A smile started to form on Talia's lips, which then gave way to a giggle, then jerky splutters that sounded like an old car revving up . . . and soon she was lying on the wooden bench, laughing hard.

The rest of us exchanged looks of surprise, then confusion . . . but soon we were all laughing even harder and louder than her. Talia had the most infectious laugh ever – we had just never heard it before. Who would have thought? Talia, who could always see the worst in everything, had managed to lift us all up. We raced each other to get changed into our football shirts and shorts and then had a fashion show, where we took votes on Who Wore it Worst before collapsing back on the benches, helpless with laughter.

Rhiannon popped her head round. 'Everything OK in there?' she said, looking curiously at us as we cried with laughter, arms wrapped round our aching stomachs.

*

We all marched out on to the pitch together, confident that, if nothing else, we would win the worst-team-strip award.

'Imogen!' cried a woman carrying a clipboard. 'What are you doing here?' She was looking straight at Rhiannon. *Imogen?*

'I'm not Imogen.'

Clipboard Lady clapped one of her hands over her mouth and with the other pulled Rhiannon in for a hug. 'I'm so sorry, Rhiannon, it's still so difficult to tell you girls apart. Who would have thought that identical twins would be so ... identical. So you're playing football again?'

'I'm coaching,' Rhiannon said. 'I hung up my football boots a long time ago.'

Clipboard Lady nodded. 'That's right, dear, no need to try and follow in your sister's footsteps and fill her rather big boots. Playing for the national women's under-nineteens squad is rather amazing, though,' she gushed. 'Tell her I said hi.'

Rhiannon nodded stiffly before moving on to the pitch.

'What was all that about?' I asked.

'About my sister, that's what.' She sighed.

'You never told us your sister was a football pro,' Charligh said.

'You didn't even tell us you had a twin, Rhi!' I said.

Rhiannon blew out. 'Well, actually, I moved two hundred miles south from Manchester to take up this make-up artists course at Bramrock College because I was hoping to move out of her shadow. Just me and my make-up brushes. I haven't played football since I was thirteen, but my sister, well – she's amazing. And she got her first cap for England on the under-nineteens squad.'

'Why did you stop?' asked Allie.

'Well, I *liked* playing, but I didn't *love* it, not like my sister did, and I was never going to be as good as her. I would have kept at it for fun, but I felt my family expected me to play as well as Imogen, so I just dropped out. But I used to help my sister train – do dummy tackles on her and be her goalkeeper when she practised shots, that kind of thing.'

I smiled. 'And that's why you're the best coach. I'm sure your sister, Imogen – I'm sure she's great and all, but maybe she wouldn't have been a professional football player without your help.

And we couldn't have got to where we are without you either.'

'Aw, don't get all soppy, kid,' Rhiannon said, but a tiny smile peeked out at the corners of her mouth.

'It's time to warm up,' said Talia briskly.

We started with a gentle warm-up jog and some stretches before we huddled together on the grass pitch. There were just two minutes left until kick-off.

'Keep the ball moving, tire them out, look for each other before you pass. Play it safe, but not too safe,' Rhiannon reminded everyone.

Windmill Villa streamed on to the pitch, eyeing us with undisguised scorn. They were from Windmill Academy, a private school on the edge of Brighton. The team was sporting a vibrant red football strip with pristine white borders, which contrasted with the worst-strip-in-girls'-football-history look that we had going on.

The referee narrowed her eyes accusingly at me and the Windmill Villa captain. I could tell she wasn't going to stand for any nonsense. 'No funny business,' she said as if to drive the point home.

She blew the whistle – *Wheeee!*

We were off!

The Villa captain started with the ball. She slid it behind to the left forward, who kicked it wide, rolling it over the sideline. Charligh ran over to take the throw-in. She held the ball straight up over her head, then hurled it straight up to Steph, who took it, slipping into her natural, swift rhythm. The Villa defender skittered up with an awkward attempt to get the ball from her. They stood facing each other: Steph stopped, her foot poised on the ball. Number 5, the tall defender, loomed near and made herself as imposing as she could, standing legs wide apart.

Steph went forward and nutmegged her – and I scooped the ball up on the right wing, dribbling round the girl who was marking me. My first touch! I felt queasy, excited and terrified all at the same time.

I ran, dodging two defenders and flicking the ball over the sweeper's head. Talia picked it up and swept it to the side; I darted a few yards to the left of the goalie, who was crouched down, lips pressed together in concentration. Just as the ball was about to swerve a few inches left of the bar, I leaped through the air – a bit like what I used to do in dance – and headed it *straight into the net*!

We scored; I scored! A current of excitement charged through the pitch. I high-fived Talia as we ran back to centre. An early goal was just the thing to get us going . . .

After two more goals, one of which was scored by me just before half-time after a perfect corner taken by Steph, the other a last-minute by Talia, it was three–nil at the final whistle.

We had a short break before we got started on our next team. Within a few seconds of play, it was clear they were going to be a piece of cake.

The Brighton Dynamos were like us when we'd first started out: clumsy with poor ball control and non-existent teamwork skills. Charligh took a throw-in, which Layla picked up and passed down to Talia who scored her second goal of the day, followed by two from me, and Steph sneaked in a goal in the final quarter. An easy win: four–nil and, two games down, we were yet to concede a goal.

'Well done, everyone,' I said as we gathered round. 'One more win and we'll definitely go through to the finals in two weeks' time.'

'We could really do this,' said Charligh in a hushed tone.

I could see Mãe, Dad and Jordan standing close together and cheering from the sidelines. Every bit of my body was aching, but I was buzzing, not just from football but also from seeing my family as we used to be. I couldn't wait to win our last game!

My doubts were fading away. Like Charligh said, we *could* do this! Looking at my family, I knew we *had* to.

21

A Slippery Situation

My team-mates lay like stranded starfish on the grass, catching their breath before our final game. I sneaked away to the pitch next to ours.

'Wait!' Charligh bellowed, running after me.

So much for a quiet getaway. I put my finger to my lips and nodded my head over in the direction of where the Cosmos were practising.

We watched, mesmerized by the tiny right forward who burned through the solid wall of defenders like a fire raging through a forest.

'That's Harriet Goldwater – *the* Harriet Goldwater,' I said, realizing our next win might not be as easy as I'd thought.

Charligh's eyes widened as we got closer. 'They're going to slaughter us,' she said.

My hope was fast sinking like a duck in quicksand.

'We can still try our best, though,' Charligh encouraged.

'I suppose,' I muttered.

We walked back in silence to join the others. Both of us knew that our best wasn't going to be good enough. I could already see the disappointed looks that Mãe and Dad would try and hide. It would confirm what they already knew: their daughter was anything but a star. So much for trying to make my mum proud. I was still a loser.

We joined the others for our pre-match stretches.

'Where did you two go?' asked Talia.

'Never mind,' I said, not wanting to spook the rest of the team.

By the thirtieth second of the match it was obvious to all of us that we had as much chance of winning as we had of pirouetting into outer space. Our opposition was swift, skilful and strong. Even speedy Steph was outrun by the player she was marking. They had a slick way of kicking the ball so it swooped at the last minute, which meant we were running about all over the place like broken puppets. A few minutes in and my red-hot lungs felt ready to burst.

Just before the end of the first half, however, Talia intercepted a lazy corner from number 1 who tried to pass to Harriet. Finally, this was it – our chance to turn things round!

'Over here!' I yelled.

Talia swung her leg as if to kick the ball, then stole a quick look at the tall, muscular girl marking me and seemed to think better of it. Lurching forward shakily, she set off by herself round the outside. I shook my head at her and waved again . . . I knew it was just a matter of time before their left defender swept in and confidently booted the ball away from Talia back on to our end of the pitch.

Whooop! cheered the Cosmos and their supporters as the whistle went for half-time. It was two–nil to them and we hadn't really even got near their goal.

We sat cross-legged on the grass, sucking all the juice we could out of the orange slices Rhiannon and Miss Williams brought over. There was a rumble overhead and I looked up. A steady shower began to fall from the dark grey sky. I jumped to my feet, kicking at the grass in frustration.

'I've had enough of playing in the rain,' I said bitterly. 'The grass is going to be a swamp by the end of this game!'

'I know,' Layla agreed, looking mournful. She wiped a glob of mud from her ankle. 'This is definitely not cute! At least it will match our yucky strips,' she said thoughtfully.

For the second time that day, we all burst out into uncontrollable laughter.

'Must be the nerves,' Dad said, looking at us all laughing. He and Mãe were smiling warmly. They had come over to watch us while Miss Williams took a break.

'You can give me some of those nerves, then,' Mãe joked. 'They look fun.'

I smiled. This was the first time I'd seen my parents have a normal conversation in ages, instead of just barking orders or throwing accusations at each other.

'Wish us luck,' I called to them when it was time for the second half.

Waiting for the start whistle, I stood face to face with Harriet. Her flaming red hair was plastered to her head and her eyes were fixed on me. I was so busy trying to work out how we Stars could turn this match around that I missed the kick-off and before I knew it the ball was whizzing past me, followed by Harriet.

I groaned. But it turned out the terrible start didn't matter, because I soon realized that, unlike us, the Cosmos *weren't* used to playing on wet grass. At their school, they were lucky enough to be able to retreat to an artificial pitch whenever the weather was bad, which meant that they were useless on the slippery, muddy grass that afternoon. Harriet nearly did the splits once she'd got a few strides past me and Naomie quickly zigzagged in and collected the ball.

The ground had soon turned into sludge and none of their forwards could stay on their feet, let alone get a shot at the goal. The Stars, on the other hand, got back into the swing of things, reverting to our original strategy: making sure we kept the ball in their half, keeping up the pressure and forcing them to run as much as possible. Their forwards and midfielders ran up to help their defenders, forming a kind of desperate wall against our fresh onslaught.

I scored our first goal after weaving in and out of three players. The rain drizzled on and, for once, I was grateful for it. It was just as Dad had said: there was a time for everything. And this was our time to show we weren't just fair-weather players.

Ten minutes after my goal, Steph sprinted down the wing, then booted the ball from just outside the circle, leaving the girl marking her sliding on the grass. The ball rolled happily into the goal as the goalkeeper stumbled backwards in a last-minute attempt to save the unexpected strike from our right mid.

The final score was two–all. Yay! So altogether we'd had two wins and a draw with the Cosmos! My heart somersaulted for joy – before I remembered, and it landed back in my stomach. I didn't want to see the look on my friends' faces when I told them . . .

Although drawing with the Cosmos was no small achievement, a draw was still a draw. To guarantee our place in the finals, what we needed was *three wins*.

'Do you want the good news . . . or the bad news?' I said. Out of the corner of my eye, I saw Rhiannon walking over with Miss Williams. I wanted to tell my team-mates myself before the adults got there, so I hurried on. 'The good news is . . . we played our best. Can you remember our first session when –'

'How could we forget? OMG, that was the worst day of my life!' Charligh said.

'The worst, really?' Allie scoffed as everyone doubled over in laughter.

I opened my mouth to add the bad news, but by this time Miss Williams had reached us and Rhiannon was there waving a yellow sheet of paper . . .

'Your golden ticket to the final!' she exclaimed. 'Isn't this exciting?'

I was speechless. I took the paper from Rhiannon and held it delicately, as if it was made from fairy dust and would disappear in a puff at the slightest touch. I read:

RESULTS – BRAMROCK STARS FC

First game: Win – 3 points
Second game: Win – 3 points
Third game: Draw – 2 points
Total: 8 points
Congratulations! You're through to the next stage.

Rhiannon explained how we'd made it to the final – only just, but we'd made it all the same. We'd managed to get through on something called goal difference. The Hove Cosmos had also had two wins and a draw, but they hadn't scored as many goals as us so we were placed above them at the top of Group B. In the other group, the winning team was the Silvertown Shiners, who had managed three wins. We'd meet them in the final, and on the same day as that match the Cosmos and the second-placed team from Group A would play to decide who was third overall in the tournament.

'What's the bad news, Jaz?' said Talia.

'Oh, er, the bad news is we'll have to wear these ugly shirts again in two weeks!' I said.

Everyone jumped and clapped and cheered, then Layla pulled us in for a group hug.

'We did it!' said Allie as we stood happily squashed together and, to my surprise, I think I saw her blinking away some tears!

'Yes, we did,' said Charligh. 'And we'll do it again.' She grinned. 'Just one more game and the trophy and medals are ours – and we'll be almost famous!'

Excited fireflies hummed in my stomach on the way back to the changing rooms, as my team-mates continued their celebrations. This was no longer just a dream. It was finally happening.

The others all went back in the minibus, but Mãe and Dad decided we would have a special family dinner to mark our win. After Mãe had dropped off Aunty Bella and driven us all home, Dad started cooking.

'Congrats, team captain! Go and get changed, *minha anjinha*, and you can tell me all about it over dinner,' Mãe said.

I sang as I washed off the mud, grass and rain in the shower. We'd done it! We were through to the final and it had been weeks – no, months – since I'd seen my parents laughing together and being, well, *kind* to each other. I'd gone from mucking around in the playground, getting shoved by the horrid boys, to being the captain of an actual team, and with my family supporting us from the sides. This called for a double celebration: the Bramrock Stars were on their way to win the trophy and Mãe and Dad were happy again. Life was certainly good once more –

Success!

22

Mãe's Back

We hadn't all sat down for dinner like this since Mãe had left. Dad had made spaghetti bolognese with vegetarian mince.

'*Linda!* That's pretty – the purple really suits you,' Mãe said, commenting on the top I had pulled on.

'And that colour really suits *you*,' Dad said to Mãe, commenting on her crimson headwrap, which she'd tied up into a big topknot.

'It's made out of the fabric for some dresses I'm working on,' Mãe said. 'I'm making all sorts, using this lovely African wax-print fabric. I've had a lot of interest on my website based on a few sample dresses I posted.'

'I'm not surprised,' Dad said.

Mãe and Dad chatted about the news. According to them, the local services were going to rack and ruin because of 'the Cuts'.

'Can you believe their proposal to collect the rubbish once every two weeks?'

'If only those politicians would use public funds for the benefit of society. I don't know what they're doing with our taxes.'

I yawned. Their conversation was boring. 'Come on, I'll wash. You dry,' I said to Jordan.

Dad's eyebrows shot up so far they were nearly lost under his thick sandy fringe. 'So let me get this straight: my daughter is offering to take the washing-up off my hands?' He leaned forward and felt my forehead. 'Just checking your temperature, pet.'

'Geroff, Dad,' I said, laughing. I swatted his hand away as I got up from the table.

I rinsed the soap suds from the dishes and handed them to my brother.

Jordan looked at me sideways. 'Why are you looking so pleased, Jaz?'

I jerked my head towards where Mãe and Dad were still sitting together at the table, a smile playing on my lips. Jordan made that face he always does when he thinks I've done something really dumb.

'Just wait and see,' I said.

'You live in the clouds, Jaz.'

Ugh. I wish he wouldn't talk to me like I was a stupid baby. He was only two years older than me!

'Wait and see,' I said again defiantly. What did Jordan know? He was all wrapped up in his music, playing the viola or going to orchestra rehearsals and concerts. I was the one doing the tough work of trying to get our parents talking again properly. And maybe now that the frostiness had melted, Mãe would start thinking of moving back in.

By the time we'd finished the dishes, my parents had moved from the dining table to the living room and were sitting in front of the telly. Mãe and Dad were on opposite sides of our big sofa. I sat down in the middle of them and the space between us all seemed wider still.

'Drew, I *said* I'd sort out the household insurance, and I will, so please stop going on about it,' Mãe said. She banged her cranberry juice down on the coffee table. The berry-red liquid spilled out over the side of the glass on to the table and landed with a few heavy plops.

'Mãe, Dad . . .' I began desperately, 'did you see how I nutmegged that girl in the Cosmos?' How had my parents forgotten that tonight was a special occasion and we were celebrating? They were *supposed* to be happy.

They continued arguing as if I hadn't spoken.

'You're all talk and no action,' Dad said with a sigh. 'We're not kids any more, Iris. You – we – we're in our forties now. I'm sorry, but it's time to grow up.'

They kept on like that until Mãe's voice reached a shrill pitch. Dad became furiously silent.

'Two wins and a draw!' I burst out, standing up suddenly.

Mãe stopped mid-sentence. Like she had just noticed I was there with them.

'Two wins and a draw,' I repeated. 'I was the team's top goal scorer and all you two can do is fight.'

Mãe looked shame-faced. She stood up and

moved towards me. 'Jaz, I'm sorry –' She reached out an arm to touch me.

A bolt of anger surged through me and I stepped back. All of this and I still wasn't good enough!

'Can't you two just be nice to each other for one day? I thought me winning those games would make everyone happy!' I wanted to keep my voice steady, but it shook.

The room went awkwardly quiet. I could hear Jordan padding softly down the stairs. I imagined him standing at his usual listening spot on the fifth step, leaning over the banister. I bet he'd be thinking, *I told you so*. And he had told me, and I'd been wrong. As usual.

'Jaz . . .' Mãe stopped. Her words hung in the air. 'I'm sorry – *desculpa* . . .' Her voice faded to silence again. She reached out for me for a hug but I shrank back, my arms hanging limply at my sides.

She looked from me and then to Dad and then back to me. 'I'm making things worse, aren't I?' she said. No one answered. 'I'm sorry. I should go now,' Mãe said softly.

I wondered what she was sorry for – sorry for leaving us behind, sorry that she clearly didn't want to come back or sorry that she and Dad had ruined tonight? I didn't know, and I didn't care. I didn't want a sorry. I wanted her.

A dot of pain spread over the left side of my head as the front door slammed. I heard her footsteps hurrying down the path.

I looked up at Dad. His mouth was all twisted up, like the way it was that time he hammered his pinkie by accident when he was building the garden shed.

'Jaz . . .' he started. 'We really are sorry. I think once you calm down we could do with a talk.'

I shook my head away from him. How could I even begin to explain how much I missed the chilly Sunday mornings watching Dad play for the Bramrock Rangers? How could I explain how I'd thought that if I sparkled on the pitch, then Dad and Mãe would focus more on me and less on tearing themselves apart? I couldn't, so I avoided his sad eyes as he gave me a hug before I ran upstairs.

Dad was good at fixing things. That's probably why he'd got his job as a carpenter for the council. The trouble was, he got sad and cross when he couldn't fix something. And I don't mean the shaky wooden side table in the hall. Things like that were easy for him. I mean the kind of invisible broken things – like families. Sometimes they fell apart too and there were no simple instructions on how to mend them. It's funny, isn't it? The things that really matter are often the hardest to put back together again.

That night, I think Dad understood that not even he could fix this.

I found myself running up the stairs, escaping to my room as fast as I could. Hurt, shame, disappointment and anger swirled around inside my head, making it spin so fast I felt dizzy. I hoisted myself up on to the top bunk, closed my eyes and curled up into a tight ball. I cried and cried until I felt like the inside of the pearly-pink shells I'd collected last summer at Camber Sands beach – rough, hollow and empty. In just a few moments the happiness of the day had been washed away like footprints in the sand. I'd worked so hard to put everything right again, but it was clear I'd failed.

I picked Kinsley up, then flung her as far away from me as I could. Our team mascot bounced against the wall and fell to the ground. Her inky black eyes stared up at me in surprise, but I didn't care any more. What help was she to the Stars? I couldn't even help our team now. Getting through to the final was probably just a fluke. Let's face it – nothing I planned ever turned out the way it was supposed to. As usual, it was me, Jaz Santos, vs. the world.

And I'd lost, *again*.

23

Whodunnit?

Have you ever felt it's nice to be with your friends without actually having to talk or listen to them? That's how I felt. As we made our way to school on Monday morning, the silence between Charligh and me was as comfortable as my old fluffy slippers. The light rain turned into a heavy downpour. By the time we arrived, we were soaked.

We usually had to wait outside in lines before the teachers let us in at nine o'clock, but on rainy days we were allowed to go straight in and wait inside the classroom.

'Oh, no one told *me* it was a dress-up-as-a-wet-poodle day,' Summer said with a pointed look in my direction. Rosie and Erica tittered.

Well, I wasn't one to argue with the oh-so-great VIPs, so I shook my head exactly like a wet poodle would do. They weren't laughing any more once my wet, clumped curls had splattered them with rain.

'Ooh, that went in my eye!' wailed Erica.

'Thanks for the shower,' said Rosie angrily.

'You're welcome,' I said with a grin.

At break-time, I got together with my team-mates. The final was just two weeks away and we decided to use every lunchtime we could to train. As usual, the boys took the football pitch over completely and Rotten Roundtree backed them up. 'They need to train for their games,' he said.

'What about us? We need to train too,' I retorted, bursting with the injustice of it all, but he just shooed us away as if we were annoying flies.

So there we were at the far end of the playground where the school waste bins were stored. It was a grim spot to practise in but we were making the best of it.

'OK, let's play one-touch kick,' I said. 'We kick the ball against the wall so it bounces back for the next player, and so on. Got it?' Everyone nodded and we got started. It was a good drill for practising kicking the ball when it's in motion and intercepting passes.

I was still upset about my parents, but by the time the bell went for the end of break, I felt some of the heavy cloud around me starting to evaporate.

'I can't wait to learn more about the exciting wonders of algebra,' I said sarcastically as I slipped in next to Charligh. It was maths with Fussy Forrest again. Double disaster. I got out my maths book and started doodling on the edges of the back page. I noticed that Rosie and Erica, who had come in from break late, had their eyes on me. When I looked up again, they were whispering behind covered mouths. I narrowed my eyes – what were they up to?

All of a sudden, Rosie marched over to Fussy Forrest and said something. Before I knew it, the teacher was beckoning me over, her whole body jerking like a malfunctioning robot.

The class went quiet.

'Why did you do this? How dare you?' she spat. She pointed at Rosie's left cheek, which had a large red mark on it.

'I didn't touch her,' I protested.

'No, maybe you didn't directly, but your football definitely did. She told me how you kicked the ball straight at her while you and the others were training.'

Steph, Naomie, Charligh and Talia all began to speak up in my defence, but Mrs Forrest shushed them. 'I don't want to hear from any of you. Rosie has told me what happened and Erica is an eyewitness.'

Eyewitness? What did she think this was – a murder mystery? I giggled. I knew I shouldn't have but I just couldn't help it.

'You never learn, do you?' Fussy Forrest said, her voice lowered to a threatening rasp. 'Well, I hope you'll find *this* funny: you and your team are banned from playing football at lunchtime.'

'What? That's not fair!' I gasped.

'No, what's not fair is your failure to take responsibility for hurting Rosie. That's disappointing and reprehensible behaviour, Jaz, but I will not tolerate bullying in this school! Actions have consequences, my girl.'

No matter how hard I tried, it seemed Fussy Forrest would find something to blame on me.

'I. Did. Not. Do. It,' I said slowly, pressing my clenched fists against my thighs on every word.

Rosie–one. Jaz–nil, I thought. I slumped back down in my chair next to Charligh.

Rosie whispered something to Zach, who guffawed loudly. 'Aww, what a shame!' he jeered. 'I know you girls need all the practice you can get too. You'll be rubbish at the final.' Summer and Rosie tittered next to him, but I noticed Erica was staying quiet. Even quieter than usual. Maybe she was upset by the whole thing – unlike Rosie, who just wanted to get me into trouble. We knew she'd made up the story about the ball hitting her face, and she knew we knew, but she just didn't care what we thought about her.

'Don't worry,' Charligh said. 'We'll just train more after school, right?'

'I'm not worrying. I'm planning,' I said grimly.

Mrs Forrest was right about one thing: actions do have consequences. They hadn't heard the last of this. None of them had.

24

Monsters Under the Bed

I spent the rest of the day trying to figure out who had hit Rosie. Was it one of the boys and she was protecting them? Or maybe she didn't know who had done it and she was just trying to put the blame on me. Who *had* done it? I wish I knew . . . *Ugh!* My head ached and spun from trying to figure it all out. And even though I'd been thinking about it for hours, I still didn't know the answer.

All I knew was that it was all dreadfully unfair and, thanks to Fussy Forrest and Ridiculous Rosie, we were banned from lunchtime training.

Those two were always ruining things, but I'd just have to let it go – for now, that is – because we had a tournament to win. I'd have to organize extra after-school training sessions in addition to the ones we already had planned since we could no longer play at lunchtimes.

On Wednesday, we all gathered at the common. Talia insisted we practise penalties; she always wanted to prepare for the worst. Allie was in goal as usual and the rest of us were doing three rounds of penalties each. Each of us had one shot each time, just like in a real penalty situation.

Steph ran up, slowing down slightly just before she booted the ball. It slammed into the goal, despite Allie's brave efforts to dive.

'Great shot,' said Naomie, clapping.

'Come on, last shot – it's your turn, Jaz,' Rhiannon said.

I picked imaginary bits of grass from my shorts and walked towards the penalty box at a snail's pace. Usually on the pitch I felt free and clear, like water. Now I ran woodenly at the ball. I closed my eyes for a second and in my mind's eye saw Dad taking the penalty and the sound of pain that rang out when he tore his Achilles' tendon. I winced as I stared at the open space behind Allie, then kicked out, aiming to get the ball in the top right corner of the goal. It bounced off the top of the crossbar, then plopped right into Allie's outstretched gloved hands. My heart sank. Everyone else had managed to get at least one shot past Allie except me. What kind of a forward couldn't get a penalty in? I tried to shake off the worry, but it crept up from my toes through all my limbs and swelled in my head.

'Jaz, are you OK?' Rhiannon said as the team began our warm-down jog round the common and I lingered behind, pulling off my shin pads.

'Sorry, Rhi, I've not practised penalties as much as I should have.'

'I wasn't talking about that,' she said. 'You seem really jumpy and distracted today.' I realized Rhiannon wasn't telling me off for my mind being somewhere else, not like Ms Morgan did. It looked like Rhiannon cared.

All my feelings crashed about inside. I was sad about Rosie's lie, which meant I couldn't do my favourite thing at lunchtime any more; angry that Rotten Roundtree and the boys and everyone else thought the boys' team was more important than ours; and disappointed that my parents couldn't sit in the same room for a minute without snapping at each other. Most of all, I was upset that nothing I did ever seemed to be quite good enough. *I* wasn't good enough –

'Have you ever been scared about something that you can't do anything about?' I began. 'So scared that you focus on something else instead? And you tell yourself that, if you can do that thing, it will make everything else better. Even though – deep down – you know it doesn't make much sense. You know, like get to fifty keepy-uppies and your parents will stop being angry all the time ... or something?' My voice had shrunk to a whisper. I felt a bit like a turtle without its shell, showing a part of myself that I usually kept covered up.

'Yeah, kind of,' said Rhiannon. 'When we were little, I was terrified of the dark whenever Imogen went on overnight football trips. So I told myself that if I didn't step on any of the cracks in the pavement, the monster under my bed wouldn't come out while she was away.'

Hearing the softness in Rhiannon's voice, I felt a lump form in my throat.

'How do you stop feeling like that?' I asked.

'Well, for me, I just forced myself to look under the bed. Then I saw that there was no monster there. It was terrifying, but facing my fear head-on was what I needed to do. You have to be brave in your own way,' Rhiannon said gently.

How could I be brave when I was filled with fear and worry? Rhiannon was being kind, but she couldn't understand. Not really. I pulled my shell back on and flashed my biggest smile to reassure her. 'Look, there's Talia waving me over,' I said as brightly as I could. 'You know how strict she is at making sure we all do the warm-down routine.' I giggled. 'I'd better join them or she'll throw the rule book at me.'

Rhiannon gave me a thumbs up as I jogged over to join my team-mates on their second lap round the common. I just wanted to try and forget about everything at home. I still had football. At least for a little while, I could forget about not being good enough, forget about the guilt I felt for missing Mum instead of feeling more grateful to my dad who was there all the time and forget about feeling angry and sad all mixed in together at Mãe for not being there.

25

Art Attack

It was the following Monday and we had a few more minutes to finish our retelling of a classical myth before we moved on to our art lesson, Miss Williams announced. I had written a modern-day version of the Greek myth about Achilles:

> Austin's mum was called Sandra. She was unemployed. She lived in Los Angeles where she had moved to make sure her son would have the best chance of becoming an

actor in Hollywood. From the moment Sandra saw Austin, with his big bright eyes, she hoped he would turn the family fortunes around. The first day she took him out in his pram, she discovered a golden lake. Then she heard a voice telling her to dip Austin in the golden lake to make him undefeatable. Sandra was very worried but the voice told her to hurry up and get on with it. She picked him up and put him in the water but she refused to let go of him because she was worried he would drown. She definitely wasn't going to let that happen! So she kept hold of his heel and brought him out of the water again really quickly. She almost thought it was a dream because suddenly Austin was dry and the lake was now dried mud and the annoying voice from nowhere had vanished.

I read my story again and nibbled the top of my pen. I couldn't think how to end it, which is how a lot of my stories went. I wrote OK at the start, and was quite good in the middle, but I *always* got stuck at the end.

'Earth to Jaz. I repeat: earth to Jaz,' said Charligh in a robot voice. 'It's time for art!' We rushed to pick our paint palettes, pencils and drawing paper to be ready for our next lesson.

'So let's recap,' said Miss Williams. 'What do we know about impressionist art? How does it differ to modern European art?'

I leaned my chair as far back as I could so my bushy ponytail brushed the front of the desk behind me. I wasn't bothered about trying to be good any more. Where had it had got me? In trouble – that's where.

'Jaz, four legs, please!'

'I've only got two,' I said.

Zach sniggered.

Miss Williams gave me a sharp look before turning her attention back to the rest of the class. 'We have the privilege of a visit by a special artist next week. He's the artist-in-residence at a gallery

I used to teach at. He specializes in impressionist art and his paintings have been exhibited all round the world. His name is André Flower Lemons.'

I spluttered loudly. What kind of name was *André Flower Lemons*?

'Grow up,' Rosie hissed.

'Today I want you to work in pairs to paint your most heroic warrior prince or princess in an impressionist style. It will be a competition: Mrs Forrest will be along at the end of the lesson to pick the winners, who will get to present their picture to André Flower Lemons.'

André Flower Lemons – *seriously*? Another giggle floated up in my throat.

'Don't let the side down,' Miss Williams warned as Charligh and I moved our desks closer together to work. We drew a princess who we called Cassandra the Courageous, but in the end she looked more like a strange-looking lumpy Barbie doll.

'Somehow I don't think we'll win,' said Charligh.

I shrugged. 'I don't think so either, unless of course Fussy Forrest isn't wearing her glasses.'

'Even if she was wearing a blindfold, she'd make sure she never let us win,' Charligh said.

'Yeah, good point.' I rolled my eyes. I could guess exactly who was going to win. Not only was Rosie pretty good at drawing, but Fussy Forrest adored her.

'OK, class, it's time for Mrs Forrest to judge your pictures. Whatever she decides, remember you're all winners.' We went up in pairs to the front of the class to present our artwork to the rest of the class. Then Mrs Forrest came in to make the final choice. We all waited in suspense as she walked ominously round the room, studying our paintings. She just couldn't resist a little smirk when she looked at Cassandra. I gritted my teeth. If anyone was the bully here, it was Fussy Forrest.

Eventually she walked back to the front of the class to make her announcement. 'The winner is . . . Amy, Queen of the Aztecs!'

'We did it! We won!' squealed Rosie and she gave Erica a hug.

'*Ugh*,' said Charligh, shaking her head in disgust. 'Theo and Neeta worked really hard on theirs and it was just as good as Rosie and Erica's, if not better. I'm not surprised they look annoyed.'

Rosie stopped bouncing up and down and gave me a look of triumph as she walked back to her seat behind me.

'Let's all give Rosie and Erica a clap, Year Six,' Mrs Forrest said warmly. I don't know if she had any kids, but if she did, I bet she wished they were all like Rosie. Everyone wanted a daughter like Rosie. No one would want a daughter like me. My own mum didn't want a daughter like me.

The clapping sounded like thunder in my ears and my head throbbed and hummed with a dull pain like angry bees were inside. I took one look at Rosie's smug smile and anger swept through me. I grabbed the paintbrush and stabbed it into the neon green paint that was still on our table. Then I marched over to Amy the Aztec and, in a frenzy of wild and bold strokes, covered her in green warpaint.

Better, much better, I thought.

I looked defiantly at Rosie. I was ready for her. I thought she might shout insults or pull my hair. Or even scurry over to her biggest fan, Fussy Forrest, to whine about me.

The worst thing was she didn't do any of those things.

The worst thing was Rosie started to cry right there in the middle of the classroom.

Have you ever done something so utterly mean and horrible that you regretted it straight away? Well, that's how I felt at that moment.

The silence in the class boomed loud. Mrs Forrest spun round in the doorway. 'What's going on?' she barked.

I felt numb as everyone stood and gaped while the deputy head dragon followed Miss Williams's gaze over to where I was standing.

'Jasmina Santos-Campbell, you get worse every day,' she said, but she looked strangely satisfied. I suppose all her predictions about me were coming true.

I kept my mouth firmly closed, certain that if I said anything it would all come out wrong. Deep down, I wanted to tell Rosie that I was truly sorry for destroying her painting. I'd only done it because everything seemed so dreadfully unfair: Mãe leaving and not coming back, even though I'd worked so hard to get to the final, and then getting blamed for doing something to Rosie that I didn't do.

What would be the point of explaining, though? Rosie would probably just glare and say

I was lying, and Mrs Forrest only expected bad behaviour from a 'bad girl'. So the words that would never come out gathered in my throat like rocks caught in a tunnel.

'Well? Nothing to say for yourself, Jasmina? That's one for the record books,' Mrs Forrest said. She leaned closer to me, her eyes slimy like a dirty garden pond. 'Your big match is in four days, isn't it? Well, I hope your friends enjoy it because you, young lady, won't be going!'

I heard my friends gasp behind me as, just like that, our championship hopes were crushed. It wasn't only the end of the football team, it was also the end of my football dream.

What had I done?

26

The End of the Dream

To make things worse, I had to spend the first ten minutes of lunch break listening to Fussy Forrest go on and on. And when she finally finished, she made me just sit there for a while 'thinking about what I had done'. By the time I reached the hall, I didn't have much of an appetite. Allie budged up to make space for me at the table. I sat down, wedged between her and Layla.

I opened my mouth to speak, but Talia jumped in first.

'I never thought you would be so unkind,

Jaz,' she said. Even Steph and Naomie wore disappointed looks and they wouldn't even meet my eyes. Guilt, sadness and regret swished around my stomach, burning inside me like a bubbling swamp.

Allie frowned. 'Why?' she asked. 'What happened? What did you do, Jaz?' The others hadn't had a chance to tell her and Layla yet.

'She vandalized Rosie's painting, right after Mrs Forrest announced it as the winner in our class competition. Rosie and Erica were going to present it to an artist called André Flower Lemons, and now it's ruined and they're really upset. So everything is spoiled,' Talia said grimly.

Layla looked shocked. 'What do you mean, *everything* is ruined?'

I stared down at my sandwich. 'Fussy Forrest said . . . I can't have the time off on Friday for the match.'

'But that's the final!' Layla cried out.

'Well done, Sherlock,' said Charligh sarcastically.

'Hey! Don't have a go at *my* friend! She hasn't done anything wrong,' Allie said. 'You two had better sort this out. We can't have got this far for nothing. I've managed to keep out of every fight since I joined this team – so why couldn't you keep out of trouble too?'

'This is Jaz's mess, not mine,' Charligh shot back. 'So she'd better think of something to fix it. Talia's right. Jaz has ruined it for everyone. So much for being *stars*!'

Hearing that from my BBF was like someone had booted me in the stomach with their football studs.

'I didn't think you liked football that much, Charligh,' I said, folding my arms.

'Well, maybe not to begin with, but I do now. We all do. We may not all be football-mad like you, Jaz, but this became our dream too, and instead you've just been acting like it's the Jaz Santos-Campbell show.'

'Well, that's better than the Charligh Gorley show,' I snapped. My empty stomach lurched. I wanted to take the words back as soon as I'd said them – why couldn't I stop making everything worse?

Charligh's jaw tightened. 'If I wanted a Charligh Gorley show, I'd have gone to the drama group's rehearsals for the Christmas panto, but I gave that up – to help *you* and the Stars! Perhaps I shouldn't have bothered, since you're too selfish to notice it's not all about you, Jasmina Santos-Campbell.'

The whole table went quiet and I had nothing to say back. I'd never seen my best friend so angry, or use my full name like that, and although her words stung, deep down I knew she was absolutely right.

Layla sniffled and hiccupped next to me. *Great! Now I've made someone else cry*, I thought as Steph passed her a tissue. The gnawing feeling in my stomach grew worse. Everyone looked miserable. The tired, disappointed looks on my friends' faces reminded me that they'd all given up something to be there at the training sessions every week. All that training, the pizza sale to get the money we'd needed for the minibus, the matches we'd played – we'd come so far. But when I decided the dream didn't matter, I'd only thought about myself.

Eventually Naomie spoke up. 'Do you know how stars are made?'

'Ugh, another science lesson,' groaned Allie.

I had to agree with her. *Talk about bad timing, Naomie!* I exhaled loudly.

'Do you, though?' Naomie insisted a little louder. She pushed her glasses up her nose.

'How are they made, then?' Layla asked through her sniffles.

'Stars are made when pockets of gas and dust within galaxies collapse. Then, once it gets really high-pressured and hot, something called nuclear fusion occurs, and all these molecules and atoms come together to form a star.'

'So? What's that got to do with anything?' said Talia coldly.

'No, wait – I get it,' said Layla softly. 'When the atmosphere gets super hot, stormy and explosive, all the bits come together to make these wonderful sparkly things we call stars.'

'Right! Doesn't that sound familiar, guys?' Naomie said.

Charligh muttered a grudging 'Maybe' in response, but Allie and Talia stared stonily ahead and didn't seem convinced. I understood, though. Kind of. This could be the best time for us to get together and shine; the best time for us to be stars. We could still do this. I just needed to figure out how.

All this time, I'd been worrying about stuff

around me that I couldn't really control – how my parents treated each other, whether the boys believed we could be as good as them, why the teachers kept thinking Rosie was the perfect student. I'd let all that take over and ruin the dream I'd had. Well, if I'd got us into this mess, then I was going to have to find a way to dig us out! I'd start by focusing on what I *could* actually change.

'I'm going to fix this,' I said firmly. 'I know I've messed everything up, but you can trust me this time. Honest.'

The iciness at our table had melted a little, but I knew words weren't enough. I had to show my team just how serious I was by what I did, not only by what I said.

That evening, after dinner, I sat on the sofa next to Dad while Jordan practised his viola upstairs.

'Fancy a bit of *Crimebusters*?' said Dad as he switched the telly on.

'Sounds good,' I said.

The first crime report was an update on a solved mystery. A mysterious person on a moped had swooped down on the Brighton Boardwalk and stolen a number of purses and wallets from unsuspecting tourists. They discovered that while the moped thief was nifty on two wheels, they weren't the world's smartest criminal. They had gone straight to Churchill Square Mall, using contactless to treat themselves. The purchases led the police straight to the thief – a local woman named Shirley Tipperstone with an eye for fashion.

'She's got a nerve,' Dad whistled, as the mall footage showed the police marching silver-haired Shirley off, while she held tightly on to her loot of shopping bags.

The second case was under investigation. It was an appeal for locals in Croydon to come forward with evidence about orange graffiti art that kept appearing on the house of a man who had recently announced he was running for election to the local council. It was a mystery to everyone in the neighbourhood, and each time it happened there was outrage in the community.

Dad frowned thoughtfully. 'This is a tricky one. I mean, who's to say it's not someone from his own campaign team doing this?'

'Why would his friends do that?' I scoffed.

'Well, think about it – the rival councillor in that ward is extremely popular with voters year on year. She does heaps for the community and her political party's official colour is orange so this graffiti obviously implicates her supporters. No one had really heard of this new political hopeful before, and now look how famous he's getting with his name splattered all over the papers each time his house is daubed in orange. Heaps of sympathy equals more votes!' Dad shrugged. He flicked to another channel as *Crimebusters* moved on to a rather gory murder investigation.

Upstairs in my room, I brought down Kinsley and a few of my other teddies from the top bunk and placed them in a circle with a small space between each of them, the same way I did with cones at football practice. I dribbled my soft squidgy mini ball between them as fast as I could, going round and round my homemade circuit.

I kept thinking over what Dad had said about *Crimebusters*. It was a real life 'whodunnit'. Then it hit me. You know when a relative gives you a really tricky, mind-boggling jigsaw that makes your brain hurt when you finally have a go at it on Christmas night? And the pieces are lying all higgledy-piggledy and nothing seems to fit anywhere, then BOOM! You get that one piece in the proper place. And – just like that – you see a clear picture of how everything else fits. That's how I felt right then. I hadn't solved the mystery for the Croydon locals, but I'd just solved a mystery much closer to home.

27

Putting the Pieces Together

The next morning, I positioned myself at the front window from where I could see everyone who walked down Half Moon Lane on their way to Bramrock Primary. Every day she went past at about the same time. Her hood was up but I could tell from her red backpack and way of walking that it was definitely her.

I opened the door and hurtled down the front path. I kept running until I was square in front of her.

Erica looked startled.

'Why did she do it?' I gasped, breathless from my short sprint.

Her face changed, but she said, 'I've got no idea what you're on about.' She fidgeted with the charm bracelet that she wore on her left arm and walked round me. Her hood had slipped halfway down her head and I could see the tips of her ears had gone pink.

'I know Rosie lied,' I insisted, walking beside her. 'And I want to know why you went along with it.'

Erica looked around, probably hoping Rosie would turn up to save her. Then she stopped. Her chin trembled and for a second I thought she was going to cry.

She held up the bracelet she'd been fiddling with. 'Rosie gave me this. It's pretty, but sometimes I don't want to wear it. But she told me to – and I know she won't be my friend if I don't do what she says –' She stopped to take a breath. Her eyes were fixed firmly on the path.

There was a long pause. Erica had barely said two words that were her own over the past couple of years. I'd got used to her being Rosie's shadow and echo.

'The rehearsals for *Spinning Alices* haven't been going well,' Erica continued. 'Rosie's worried about remembering all the steps and doing it exactly like Ms Morgan said. Her mum has been really cross and grumpy with her lately because everything's about the new baby. Rosie says the only way she gets any attention is if she says someone is being horrid to her at school. We saw you practising near the bins and Rosie decided we'd have a go at football too after you all left. She said anything you lot can do we can do better. Except when I kicked the ball it bounced against the wall and into Rosie's face. I didn't mean to do it.'

I'd been bluffing – I hadn't known for certain who was responsible but Erica had just confirmed my suspicions. She looked up cautiously. For the first time, I noticed her eyes didn't look so empty. They looked kind and thoughtful. Maybe there was more to Erica than being Rosie's echo. She hadn't actually said sorry for setting me up, but I supposed this was about as close to an apology as I would get.

'What are you going to do?' she asked. I hated what she and Rosie had done, but I had to admit Erica had been brave to tell me the truth at last.

I shrugged. Before Erica's confession, I'd had a plan of exactly what I was going to do when I found out who the culprit was. I was going to grab them by the arm, march them down to Fussy Forrest's office, and make sure they gave me a great big sorry. Now, though, I wasn't so sure. Things weren't exactly as I'd thought – they were more complicated. I felt sorry for Rosie. I knew what it was like to feel ignored by your parents and feel like you had to do something to make them notice. Of course, Rosie and I had had very different ideas of what to do about it, but we were still alike in many ways.

Erica and I walked on together in silence until we reached the school gates. Everyone had already gone in from the playground.

'You go first, Erica,' I said. 'I don't want Rosie to give you a hard time for walking with me.'

Erica gave me a grateful smile, then she scurried ahead of me through the main doors, where the latecomers had to go in. I counted thirty footballs before I followed her. Now I just had to figure out what to do next.

Our first lesson was maths – yuck! But Miss Williams was taking us today instead of

Mrs Forrest. Somehow she made even long division and algebra interesting, so it wasn't too bad.

When the bell rang for break, I tried to tell Charligh I would catch up with her later, but she marched out ahead of me. My best friend was barely speaking to me. To be fair, can you blame her? It seemed I'd ruined a lot more than just our chance of bringing home the trophy.

I waited until everyone was gone and the wild chatter and shouts had faded to silence down the corridor. Miss Williams smiled as I approached her desk. She looked as if she had been expecting me

'How are you, Jaz?' The warm kindness in her voice made my eyes fill with tears. I blinked them away.

'Honestly, miss? We all worked so hard to get to the tournament and then the final, but now I've gone and ruined our football dream. No final, no trophy and maybe no team. I don't know if the Bramrock Stars will ever want to play football with me again. Everything's a mess!'

Miss Williams pulled out the stool at the side of her desk. 'OK, Jaz, take a deep breath and let's try and work out what "everything" is.'

I sat down on the stool and rested my elbows on the edge of her desk. 'What am I supposed to do without football and without my friends?' I asked. 'And my parents hate each other. They don't talk any more – they just shout. Dad kind of mopes around, trying to avoid talking about it; and my mum, well ... she seems to have forgotten that I even exist. They ruined my celebration last week after we got into the finals, and then Mrs Forrest blamed me for something horrible I didn't do, and then I got into trouble for something really horrible that I did do –' I breathed in heavily and blew out. Hard.

My teacher looked at me calmly. 'Parents disagree sometimes, Jaz – maybe it even seems all the time – but that doesn't mean they hate each other. And I know they certainly haven't forgotten about you.'

I managed a tiny smile. I wasn't convinced. Still, I wanted to make amends with Rosie. 'No matter what, though, I shouldn't have taken it out on Rosie's painting,' I went on. 'Even if it is unfair that she seems to win everything and get her own way *all* the time. I reckon with a bit of work I could make her picture as good as new again.'

Miss Williams looked thoughtful, then she bent down and rummaged in her desk drawer, before reappearing with a long watercolour palette. Next, she brought Rosie's painting out from the art cupboard and placed it on her table, moving her endless stacks of books to the side.

She handed me a long, thin paintbrush. 'I think you can do it too,' she said.

I made slow and steady short strokes, blending and mixing the colours, shading, covering, creating. I worked like that for the whole of break-time. Miss Williams sat alongside me, adding a stroke here and there and tracing pencil lines for me until it was finished.

'I think Rosie is going to love it as much as I do,' she said.

I glanced up at the clock. There were a few minutes left before the others came back in from break.

'One more thing –' I grabbed a palette of six bold colours and, dipping the paintbrush into them, I blended and painted some more. 'Amy, Queen of the Aztecs has a stormy background, but I thought here at the top we could have a rainbow . . . because, you know, there's often a rainbow after the storm.'

Miss Williams nodded. 'There certainly is.'

'I know I can't fix everything,' I said as we moved the painting back into the cupboard to dry, 'but at least I can fix something.'

As everyone spilled back into the room, Charligh stopped to speak to me.

'What were you doing in here, Jaz?'

'It's a long story,' I said. 'I'll tell you all later.'

'Whatever.' She paused. 'We missed you at break, by the way.'

'I missed you too,' I said, my smile stretching from ear to ear. Perhaps I hadn't lost my BBF after all.

At home-time, Miss Williams asked Rosie, Erica and me to stay behind. Rosie stared as I brought out the painting. She hadn't said a word to me since I'd spoilt it in our art lesson.

'Rosie,' I said, 'I'm really sorry for ruining your painting. Honest.'

A shocked smile spread over Rosie's face as she saw the restored painting and realized what I had done. 'It's not exactly the same, but it's brilliant! What did you do, Jaz?' Without waiting for an answer, Rosie bent forward and kissed the air on both sides of my face, the way she told us they did in Paris – 'Mwah! Mwah!'

'So . . . you like it, then?' I said.

'I love it!' Rosie said with a click of her fingers. 'Do I still get to give this to André Flower Lemons, miss?'

'Of course, Rosie. Well done. You really deserve this.'

'So now, when we meet the famous artist, we can tell him about an important moment in art history,' Rosie said. She paused for dramatic effect. 'Our masterpiece was nearly destroyed by the class terror,' she declared in a loud whisper to Erica, with a sidelong look at me.

I couldn't help but roll my eyes as the VIPs made their way out of the class. Maybe Rosie wasn't completely awful after all, and she *did* have feelings, but she was still a Royal Pain.

28

Confessions

There was a thoughtful pause on the phone after I'd told Mãe all about Rosie and Erica setting me up, how horrible I'd been when I ruined their picture, and how much playing football with the Stars meant to me.

'I don't know when I'll get to play football again, Mãe.'

She had listened patiently as I'd gone through everything – well, nearly everything. I hadn't plucked up enough courage to tell her about my very worst fear: that somehow all of this – not just the trouble at school, but the bickering between my parents too – was somehow my fault. I wasn't brave enough to say that there was something wrong deep inside me that meant that I kept ruining everything around me.

I could hear her smile at the other end. 'Do you remember playing Jenga?' she said.

'Mm-hmm,' I said slowly, wondering why Mãe was talking about games we played at Christmas.

'If you make one wrong move with your piece, then all your hard work comes tumbling down. Life isn't Jenga, though, *anjinha*. Just because you make one mistake, it doesn't always mean your entire dream is ruined.'

'I hope not,' I said. 'Everything feels better when I'm dribbling the ball round players and booting it into goal. I could play every day and still not get enough of it.'

'What you've achieved with the Stars – it's all building blocks for something bigger. I remember the first time I saw your dad roll a ball to you in the front room, and even though you'd only been walking for a few weeks you kicked it back with as much determination as a toddler could. We've always known you were going to be a super striker!'

The smile in her voice faded a little as she continued, 'I'm sorry I ruined your celebration after the match the other day . . .' Her voice trailed off.

'It's OK, Mãe.' I wanted to say more, but I wasn't sure what.

'Anyway, let's have a celebration this weekend in Brighton,' Mãe said.

I giggled. 'Celebrate what? Forfeiting the final on Friday?'

'No, celebrating not letting go of our dreams, even when we fail and make the wrong decisions!'

'Can we get our special dessert from Mr Henry's diner?' My stomach rumbled as I thought of the gooey, chocolatey fudge dessert.

'Deal!' said Mãe.

'At least I don't have to wear that awful strip,' I said. I was only joking, of course. I'd have loved to bring that golden trophy back home, no matter what I was wearing, but perhaps it just wasn't meant to be. And who knows whether the Stars would have won, even if we did play? The competition was so tough.

'There's always next year,' I said, trying to sound cheerful . . . *If my friends ever trust me again*, I thought.

29

A Surprise

On Wednesday, I stood in front of Fussy Forrest's door, trying to keep the nerves away by counting footballs. *Eleven footballs, twelve footballs, thirteen footballs . . .* On my way back in from break, the teacher on playground duty had passed me a note asking me to report to Mrs Forrest's office before I went back to the classroom. I was racking my brain, struggling to remember what else I'd done wrong that I'd not already been punished for. I finally plucked up the courage to knock at the door and, to my surprise, it was

Miss Williams I heard saying, 'Come in!' I stepped inside, still feeling queasy.

I had no idea what I'd done now, but with all the trouble I'd been in lately, I figured it was better to apologize sooner rather than later. 'Sorry, I didn't mean it,' I blurted out.

'Didn't mean what?' Miss Williams asked, smiling gently. 'You aren't the one who's done anything wrong here. If anything, I think *we* owe *you* an apology – and that's why we've called you in here.'

I looked from Miss Williams to Mrs Forrest, who sat with her arms crossed and her lips pursed.

'*You* owe *me* an apology . . .? But for what?' I gasped.

Miss Williams cleared her throat and looked at Mrs Forrest, who still had a pinched sort of look on her face. Then Mrs Forrest sighed. 'Jasmina, it's just as Miss Williams says. It appears that we may have . . . that we did actually get the wrong end of the stick about who exactly kicked that ball at Rosie. I suppose . . . er, I mean, we were . . . um, wrong to punish you –' She stopped, but she looked as uncomfortable as I'd felt when I'd walked in.

Miss Williams continued. 'This morning, Rosie, encouraged by Erica, came in with her mum and confessed everything. Rosie is really keen that you be allowed to play in the final, and her mum spoke about the restoration of the masterpiece as a monumental piece of school art history.' Her mouth twitched like she wanted to laugh. 'Of course, we had to come to our decision independently, and I'm pleased to tell you that we have reinstated your permission to go to the football final on Friday. I think we've all learned our lesson about looking at things with fresh eyes and not being so quick to judge.' I could see Fussy Forrest squirming as Miss Williams gave her a sideways look.

Mrs Forrest then droned on for a while about the 'offending pupils' (that would be Rosie and Erica) being 'appropriately punished', but I wasn't even really listening any more. The thrill rushing through me wasn't about the VIPs being in trouble. I was just over the moon that I was going to the final! I was pleased too that the truth was out. I don't know how Erica did it, but she must have found the courage from somewhere to get Rosie to do the right thing. It seemed like she did have her own mind after all.

My insides tingled with sparks of shocked delight. How could a week that had begun so horribly be ending so brilliantly?

30

All In

'In. Out. In. Out.' At lunch, Talia pretended to bang her forehead on the table in frustration. 'This isn't the hokey-cokey, you know,' she said sternly. 'Let's get this straight. So, you're definitely back in the team and we can go along to win this tournament on Friday, and live happily ever after?'

We all burst out laughing. Only Talia could sound so grouchy about doing a huge thing like bringing the trophy back. That was just Talia, though – I could tell that she was really excited, even if she didn't sound it!

We all were. The deafening cheer that had gone up from our table when I announced the news was enough to confirm that, and also enough to have Fussy Forrest come over and tell us to be quiet.

'So anyway, Jaz . . . what was that you were saying about us having no chance in the tournament again?' Charligh said.

We were gathered at our usual spot at lunchtime and Charligh was still rubbing it in. She spooned a dollop of thick chocolate mousse from the tiny plastic tub. It trembled as she waited for my reply with her spoon poised in mid-air.

'OK, OK! I was wrong,' I admitted.

Charligh stood up and cleared her throat. 'On behalf of all the Stars, I would like to accept this apology, as feeble and pitiful as it was.'

I rolled my eyes as everyone laughed. I was so glad to have my BBF back that I didn't really mind the teasing. After I'd apologized to everyone, I shared with my team-mates how sad I'd been feeling about my parents' separation and how everything felt so weird at home now. I told them about Rosie framing me, but left out the bit about why she'd done it. I decided it would hurt Rosie too much if everyone knew her reasons.

Steph gave me a big warm hug, and Charligh reminded me that I could always talk to her. Then Allie shared a bit about how she felt living with just her mum; she barely saw her dad, she said.

It made me feel a lot better to be honest with my friends and also to know that some of them really understood a little about how I was feeling.

'So six o'clock at the common?' I said.

Everyone said they would be there. This was our final chance to sharpen our skills right before our big day.

Rhiannon and I led the warm-up. We jogged round the common a few times. The early-evening grass was slightly frozen and crunched under our heavy steps.

We began with our usual ball-control drill, where we all lined up to dribble the ball as fast as we could between the tightly spaced cones. Next, we did shuttle runs, jogging one way between the cones, then doing a quick sprint back.

'Enough,' gasped Charligh. 'Let's move on to toe traps now.' She winked at me and nodded towards Talia.

'We still have thirteen minutes left of this,' Talia said.

You could always count on Talia to be drill sergeant and keep things according to plan.

After an hour of practising step-overs, keepy-uppies and flick-ups, we sat down with Rhiannon to talk about what else we could work on. This used to be super awkward, because none of us wanted to listen to what we had to improve on. Things were different now, though; we were brave enough to hear not only about our strengths, but about the bits that really did need more work. How else could we get better if we weren't honest about our performance? I'd always thought honesty was just about not lying, but I realized it was more than that. It was also about speaking the truth when it mattered.

Naomie went first. 'We're great at passing when we're close to each other,' she said.

'But Charligh and I aren't so great at passing down the midfield into the goal box,' said Steph.

'The defence – Charligh and Naomie – are strong when it comes to tackling, but we need to form a solid wall when it comes to free kicks,' Allie added.

'We, or at least *I*, need some practice on penalties.' I grimaced. I hated penalties. I always kicked the ball all wonky under pressure.

We talked a little bit more about our weaknesses and strategies for the final. We were dreaming a big dream, but also had to be realistic and focus more on what we could achieve in a short time. Mind you, if we'd been too realistic, we would never have imagined we'd be where we were now.

At the end of training, we huddled round Miss Williams and Rhiannon to hear the instructions for Friday. We had received special permission from Mrs Rivers to leave school at morning break so we could travel to the final in a coach. The school had already paid for it for the boys' team, but, since they'd got knocked out at the first stage of their tournament, they wouldn't be needing it. Mrs Rivers didn't see any reason why we shouldn't use it instead, and the coach company hadn't minded changing the booking so we could have it for our match on Friday.

Dad walked over from where he'd been watching at the side of the common. 'I have a surprise for you,' he said. He rummaged around in his huge duffel bag and pulled out the most beautiful football shirt I'd ever seen. It was deep violet with a black collar. A set of three purple stars had been embroidered above a round emblem that read BRAMROCK STARS FC. Then he pulled out some matching purple football socks and shiny purple shorts.

'I LOVE THIS!' Charligh bellowed.

'We're going to look so cool,' gushed Layla. 'Where did you get these, Mr Campbell?'

'We must thank Jaz's mum for these,' he said.

My eyes filled with hot, happy tears, and all I could see was a blurry mass of purple in front of me when Steph handed me mine. As I blinked my tears away and turned it round, I could see it had the number three on it. We all had numbers on our shirts. We were a proper team and these were ours!

'How?' I gasped, finally able to speak.

'Your mum spoke to the PTA and, well, they pulled a few strings to get some money to purchase a new strip, then she worked all night sewing those beautiful star logos on,' Dad said.

I watched as my team-mates picked out their shirts and shorts. I knew, win or lose, that one thing was for sure – '*Nos somos as Estrellas Bramrock!*'

'What does that mean?' asked Allie, clutching her long-sleeved goalie top.

'We are the Bramrock Stars!'

When Dad and I got home, I had a video chat with Mãe. She'd been invited to present her new designs at a major fashion festival in London, so she wouldn't be there the next day, but Dad had agreed to record all the best bits from the match for her. I put my shirt and shorts on so she could be the first one to see me wearing them, and her face lit up.

'Don't forget that passion and love you have for the game and what your football dream is really all about,' Mãe said before we said goodbye. 'You can do it, *anjinha*. Shoot for the stars! And I'm not just talking about Bramrock Stars FC!'

I knew winning wouldn't bring Mãe back or make my dad stop frowning and worrying, however much I wished it could. I still felt a tiny pang about it, but it wasn't as deep or as sharp a pain as before. I pushed those thoughts out of my head and then excitement, hope and nerves bounced around me like the balls we kicked about at training.

Only two more nights until the final! The Bramrock Stars would be on that pitch, fighting for the championship trophy. We were a team of stars who were ready to make our dream our reality. Except there was just *one* more thing I needed to face first . . .

31

A Dream Recipe

I faced Dad as he guarded our makeshift goal. The garden lamps cast a cool blue light over the grass and Dad's shadow loomed over the football I'd placed a few steps in front of me. I ran towards it and booted it . . . right into Dad's hands.

'Try again, princess,' he said encouragingly.

I did. And he saved it. Again. I'd been outside for ten minutes, practising penalties with Dad after dinner, and I hadn't got even one goal in. I wanted to walk away and just hope for the best tomorrow – that it wouldn't go to penalties, and that we would, by some miracle, defeat the Shiners anyway. But I'd been thinking about what Rhiannon had said, about looking under the bed and facing your monster, and I knew I had to face my fear of penalties. I'd stood up to the VIPs, Bully Boy Bacon and all the other doubters who'd said we couldn't make it this far, but still my biggest monster remained. It wasn't under my bed: it was a thing that lived inside my head – my fear that I wasn't good enough, that I had to keep proving myself to everyone, that I was a disappointment. So, even though penalties still made me turn to jelly, I was ready to stare that fear in the face. Courage wasn't not being afraid. It was about standing up to your fears.

I tried again and again, and again, until – *finally!* – I got one past Dad. I knew he hadn't just let me have it. He'd dived across the goal to stop it, but the ball had sneaked in at the far right corner.

'Good shot! That left foot got me,' Dad said, holding his hands up in defeat.

I whooped and did a victory lap round the garden. I'd lost count of how many shots at goal I'd missed before my last one had gone in, but I'd realized something important: that I wasn't so afraid any more. All those times people had said I was lazy and didn't try hard enough or couldn't stay out of trouble – maybe they'd been wrong about me. Maybe I'd just been afraid. It all started to make sense now, like a jigsaw coming together. It had been scary, trying to do my very best all the time when I'd just thought I was going to fail, when I thought one mistake would be the end of everything, but I'd kept going, shot after shot after shot, failure after failure, and that had been my success.

'Dad, remember what you said about wishing life came with a recipe so you could make sure it would turn out just right? Well, this morning I made a recipe for the final –' I narrowed my eyes, trying hard to remember – 'a spoonful of courage, heaps of love, and a cup of hope. And even then you can't be sure things will turn out the way you want, but at least you'll know you've done your best.'

Dad eye's crinkled. For a second, I couldn't tell whether he wanted to laugh or cry. I don't think he did either. He leaned over and ruffled my hair. 'Come on, Jaz, it's time tomorrow's player of the match went to bed.'

32

Here We Go!

'Wasn't it frightening when Fussy Forrest stretched her lips over her teeth and wished us good luck?' Charligh said on the coach.

'I think she was trying to smile,' Talia said thoughtfully.

Charligh shuddered. 'Hopefully she won't do *that* again.'

A few pupils from Years 5 and 6 had been allowed to come along to support us. There was Olly, Theo, Sophia-Grace, Amarachi and Neeta from Year 6, and the K triplets from Year 5, who were eager to see the first girls' team from Bramrock Primary in action. Miss Williams and Mrs Tavella sat in the front seats, across from Rotten Roundtree and Mrs Rivers. We waved goodbye to the rest of Years 5 and 6 who were cheering us on from the playground as the coach pulled out. The VIPs were nowhere to be seen because Rosie and Erica were in detention as a punishment for telling fibs. After they'd confessed about the football accident, we'd unofficially called a truce with them, but I still felt a bit wary of Rosie. Her halo wasn't quite so firmly over her head any more, but it hadn't been knocked off completely.

Of course, Zach and his mates stood scowling in the crowd because they didn't like that the Bramrock *Stars* were going to the final.

Charligh blew kisses at them. 'Look at all our fans!' she called. 'We're the Stars and we can't let them down!'

Miss Williams had shared the timetable for the day with us earlier. There were going to be two matches: our game against the Silvertown Shiners to decide who would be first and second in the tournament, and another game to decide which team got third place.

Talia sighed. 'I'm worried about our opponents,' she said. 'I think we'll find it's the Silvertown Shiners who are the stars today. They're such a strong team! I feel like hanging up my football boots already.'

'Look,' said Steph encouragingly. 'We didn't think we'd make it this far, but we did. So who knows? Maybe we'll surprise everyone – including ourselves – again.'

'I've checked their record, though,' said Naomie. 'Their success rate is one hundred per cent. They've won every match they've played this season.'

Allie shrugged. 'So? We'll thrash them anyway.'

'Sure, we'll be great,' I said, hoping I sounded more convincing than I felt.

The coach sped along and everyone settled down for the thirty-minute journey. Soon Talia was immersed in a game of chess on her phone. She tutted loudly each time the app outsmarted her. Allie drummed on the back of the seat in front of her, which unfortunately was mine, and

Charligh treated us to a performance of 'We are the Champions' in the style of an opera singer, singing a bit louder than any of us would have liked and dismissing Karina's suggestion that it might be rather early for a victory chant.

I wondered how Mãe's fashion event was going in London. Deep down, I wished she was coming to see me play. Waves of nerves surged through my stomach and up into my chest. It seemed that bit scarier that we'd have to face the Shiners without her there.

By the time we arrived at the sports ground, our nerves were as taut as Jordan's newly strung viola and we filed silently off the coach. The final was being held on the playing fields of a high school in Brighton. We made our way to the large changing rooms, which had huge steel lockers and pinewood benches.

Getting changed into our smart new football shirts and shorts made us feel a bit more of a real team. No longer were we that ragtag bunch of girls who'd struggled to do a simple pass. Now the Bramrock Stars FC were serious contenders. We were here to win that trophy! I slipped my shin guards on under my thick purple socks and tied the laces of my football boots tightly. Finally, the Stars were ready.

We gathered at the side of the artificial pitch, ready to start our warm-up. I looked over at the Shiners who wore blue-and-grey striped shirts with steel-blue shorts. It looked like they had brought their entire school as well as all their mums, dads, brothers, sisters, aunties, uncles and grandparents. Perhaps their first, second and third cousins too? In contrast, in addition to the small group of supporters who came with us in our coach, we had Dad, Aunty Bella, Mrs Gorley, Mr Osei and Mrs Hussani.

'Is it just me, or does this fancy new strip not half make you sweat?' Allie said, tugging at her collar as she did a hamstring stretch.

'No, it's not the strip that's making us sweat,' Layla said, her eyes widening as she stared across at the huge crowd behind the Shiners.

One of the Shiners' mums came over in our direction. I looked at her wobbling on her incredibly high stiletto heels. *If this was a grass pitch, she'd get stuck*, I thought, giggling inside. She had custard-yellow hair pinned up in a beehive style.

'Hello, Bramstar Rocks,' she said.

Allie scrunched her face up as if she smelled something rotten.

'It's the Bramrock Stars, actually,' Talia said.

Beehive ignored her and then pointed slowly at me, her finger travelling close to my chest. I stepped back, nearly crashing into Steph.

'Aw, sorry – I didn't mean to scare you, darling,' she said, her mouth curving smoothly up into a smile that didn't reach her eyes. 'You're the captain, aren't you? I was just admiring your team badge. How . . . cute,' she cooed.

Miss Williams came over and extended her hand. 'How do you do?' she said. 'I'm Miss Williams, class teacher and team manager of the Bramrock Stars.'

'Mrs Chatton, mother of the Shiners' forward Victoria Chatton,' she replied. She looked Miss Williams up and down, but didn't shake her hand. 'I hope you don't mind, but I want to tell the Rocks about their opponents, the Silvertown Shiners. We've won the championship in our local league twice in a row and this win will make it a championship hat-trick. Most of our girls have been playing for years, and during the holidays most of them attended an *amazing*, and rather *expensive*, football camp.'

'OK, thanks for that, Mrs Chatter,' said Miss Williams calmly, 'but now the Bramrock Stars have to get on with some last-minute training. May the best team win!'

Beehive glared at her. 'It's Chat*ton*, thank you very much.'

Miss Williams smiled sweetly but didn't apologize for her mistake. It didn't look as if Victoria's mum was going to move.

'It was lovely to meet you, Mrs Chatton,' I said, crossing my fingers behind my back.

Allie's eyes blazed at Mrs Chatton as she strutted off, leaving my friends looking a bit like the deflated footballs you see lying by the side of the pitch. We'd been stung. Beehive had pierced holes in our bubbles of confidence. We'd get totally flattened if we didn't pump ourselves back up.

Then I spotted Rhiannon jogging over to us.

'You made it!' I cried.

Rhiannon greeted each of us with a high five. She was wearing a long grey padded jacket and black suede trainers. 'Molly let me swap my shift,' she said. 'I'm on a full day tomorrow – up early on a Saturday, thanks to you guys! It's worth it, though. I can't wait to see you win that seven-a-side trophy today.'

Allie sighed heavily. Rhiannon noticed our dejected looks, and looked over towards Mrs Chatton. 'Oh dear, she's got to you already, hasn't she?'

I nodded.

'She's got an older daughter, Belinda, who played against Imogen in the Summer Football Academy trials, and she did the same to us too. Do you want to know why Victoria's mum tried to put the frighteners on you?'

'Yes. Why?' said Charligh.

'It's because she's heard all about the Bramrock Stars,' said Rhiannon. 'She's trying her best to scare you because you're the only thing that's standing in the way of the Shiners getting the trophy. She only used to do that to the teams she thought were a real threat. If she thought the Shiners could just flatten the opposition, she never used to bother at all.'

'Really?' I said, feeling a bit more hopeful.

'Really,' said Rhiannon firmly. 'Now, I don't want to hear one more word about Mrs Chatton.'

'I wasn't bothered by her anyway,' blustered Allie.

'Of course you weren't,' Rhiannon said with a wink. 'Now, come on! Let's finish our warm-up!'

33

Fair Play

A short while later, we stood poised in our starting positions, etching the faces of the players we were going to be marking into our memories. Many of the high-school students had spilled out of their classes and were gathered around the pitch. It was the biggest crowd I'd ever played in front of. From our school playground, to the common, and now to this huge crowd ... I was buzzing with excitement. One day I could even be out on the pitch at Wembley, playing in a Women's Super League final, or scoring goals for England on a pitch anywhere in the world! I could sense the tension, the Stars' silent nerves and the Shiners' loud confidence as our opponents sized us up – and felt a thrill from it all. This was it!

The whistle blew. We were off!

Jilly Hutchinson, the Shiners' captain and top scorer, powered down the centre. Charligh made a brave attempt to stop her, but Jilly swerved, with a dummy kick to the left, then a dodge to the right. I could see why she was their star player. Jilly played so smoothly, with the confidence of someone who only had one option, and that was to win. After slipping past Layla and then Allie, who had scrambled out in front of the goal, Jilly booted the ball at full pelt. I held my breath, watching its journey . . .

It sailed several inches above the crossbar, and her team-mates groaned.

Steph clapped, as if waking us all out of the stunned trance we'd fallen into. 'Come on, Stars!' she urged. 'Let's do this! Keep the ball up at their end!'

Charligh kicked the ball back out. Layla scooped it up from the left and pushed it up to Talia, who instinctively searched for me in the centre, where I was waiting for her. I steadied the ball under my foot, spun round, then ran wide of their left defender, who was confused that I was now at Talia's side.

Talia moved ahead of me until she was positioned near the goal – where she was immediately surrounded by three Shiners. She skipped a few steps wide of the goal and the defenders all followed her.

Seizing my opportunity, I flicked the ball into the far left corner of the goal. Taken by surprise, the Shiners' goalkeeper dived at the last second . . . the ball connected with her fingertips and was deflected into the back of the goal.

A loud cheer went up from our supporters and I heard Aunty Bella yelling, '*Gol!*'

On the pitch, we clapped softly, however. We were still so full of a mixture of tension and disbelief that we were reluctant to celebrate properly until we'd achieved what we wanted and won the whole match. Still, it did feel good! I allowed myself to enjoy the moment just for a little while and I inhaled deeply as I watched the figures changing on the scoreboard. One–nil to Bramrock Stars!

The ball went back to the centre, and this time it felt different. Before, we'd been testing each other out. Now the air was charged with an explosive tension. The Shiners weren't happy that we'd made such a bold attack so early in the game. The adrenalin pumped through me, making me more focused than ever. It was a different kind of energy than before, when I'd felt stressed and foggy-headed, struggling with the weight of everything. I glanced around at the others. My team-mates looked just like I felt – a magical cocktail of excited, happy and scared. We could do this . . . couldn't we?

I looked over at Dad, who was cheering loudly, and I touched the embroidered star logo on my shirt, feeling all the hard work and love that Mãe had put into every stitch, and it was like the Mãe-sized gap was gone. *Don't forget that passion and love you have for the game and what your football dream is really all about.* She was right. Maybe winning the trophy wasn't going to bring her back, but I had a dream and it mattered. Before, I'd nearly destroyed my dream, and everyone else's, by letting my worries about my parents take over. Now I had another chance. My goal as team captain was to play the best game I'd ever played and to help my team-mates do the same too.

The whistle blew and we were off again. The Shiners didn't waste any time and booted the ball from inside the circle. Allie leaped across the goal entrance, saving a strong shot from Jilly towards the side of the net. Charligh caught the ball on the rebound and pushed it up to me. I sped down the edge of the pitch, but their number six, a broad-shouldered girl, appeared out of nowhere, blocking my route down the right wing as I tried to ensure a follow-up goal to take the score to two for us. She had a determined look on her face and I felt a short, sharp pain in my shin where she was kicking me.

'Ow!' I cried. I deftly shuffled the ball from one foot to another, determined not to lose possession of it. 'What do you think you're doing?'

'Um, kicking you?' She took another swipe at my left leg. I winced, and she stole the ball away, blasting it back down towards the wingers.

'Did you see that?' I shouted at the referee, exasperated. She shrugged; either she hadn't seen it or she didn't care.

The Shiners kept up the pressure like that for several minutes, their tackles growing more vicious in their effort to take control of the game, but each attempt by their defenders to pass the ball down to Jilly was intercepted by Steph.

Jilly looked increasingly frustrated. When Steph pushed the ball up to Talia, Jilly swung her foot hard and high with unmistakable ferocity. I watched in horror as her boot connected with Steph's ankle and Steph let out a moan and sank to the ground.

34

Achilles' Heel

The first-aid officer asked us all to step back to give Steph some air.

'I'm OK,' Steph said, but her face was scrunched up in pain.

'Don't worry; she's in good hands,' the first-aid man said. He knelt down and wiggled her left ankle.

'Wrong ankle,' Steph winced.

Naomie grimaced and looked doubtful as the man turned his attention to Steph's right ankle.

Dad had come over to us. 'You'll be OK, Steph,' he said. 'Mrs Rivers has given your mum a ring, and you know what they say – it's the best players who are the first to go down.'

Steph attempted a smile, but then she just burst out crying all over again. It was dreadful seeing her like this. She was the one who always looked after everyone and made sure we were all OK.

Mrs Rivers looked even more frazzled than usual. 'Is it broken?' she asked.

'We won't know for sure until we get an X-ray, but in all likelihood what we have here is a broken ankle, in my humble opinion,' First-Aid Man said, sounding anything but humble.

The Shiners smirked as Steph hobbled off with Miss Williams and First-Aid Man.

'Send your sub on before you take the free kick,' said the ref briskly.

'But we don't have one,' I replied.

'Don't have one?' she echoed, shaking her head.

'We didn't expect to be the victims of foul play,' said Charligh defensively.

'I take it you're new to this?' said the referee. 'Next time, come prepared with substitutes . . . two of 'em! You'll just have to carry on playing with six players. And, as for you –' she turned to

Jilly – 'yellow card! Pull a stunt like that again and your team will also be one player down.'

We trudged back out on to the pitch, anxious about Steph and despairing of our chances of winning with only six girls on our team. It should have been a red card for the Shiners; it was definitely what Jilly deserved. Still, I knew better than to even try and argue with the ref's decision.

Talia took the free kick. It was picked up by Layla in midfield, but almost immediately the ball ended up back in the possession of our ruthless opposition. The Shiners weren't ashamed, not one bit. And they seemed even hungrier to win now. Realizing their advantage, they were playing harder and rougher than ever.

Allie was incredible, saving five goal shots in a row. Then just before half-time, when we were all utterly exhausted, everything seemed to happen at once. Jilly moved in and headed the ball towards the goal, the ball twirled flamboyantly to a stop inside the net, the referee blew hard on her whistle to signal the end of the first half – and the Shiners had got their equalizer.

We slumped off to the side of the pitch, our

chests heaving and our spirits low. I dropped to the ground, resting back on my elbows.

Miss Williams and Rhiannon came over with the half-time oranges and water.

'How is everyone feeling?' asked Rhiannon.

'Like this is the football equivalent of checkmate,' Talia said dejectedly.

'Devastated,' said Charligh. She clasped her heart theatrically.

Miss Williams nodded. 'They're stronger, tougher and more experienced than us.'

'Hey! I thought you were on our side, miss,' Allie said.

'I *am* on your side. That's why I'm telling you this. You have to fight back as a team and you can beat them. I'm just reminding you that your strengths may be different from theirs.'

Miss Williams didn't really know much about football, but I reckoned she was on to something. Every team was different. If we couldn't beat the Shiners at their own game, we had to beat them at ours.

'They're super confident,' said Allie. 'I don't know where they get it from. They ain't even that good, except for the fancy footwork.' She huffed.

'Confident? I think *arrogant* is the word you are looking for,' said Naomie.

'That's it!' I said, sitting up straight.

'That's what?' said Naomie.

'Their Achilles' heel. Arrogance. That's how we are going to win. We're going to use their arrogance to our advantage.'

Five blank faces looked at me.

'Remember the story of Achilles, the hero from the Greek myths?' I said.

'Yeah,' Naomie said. 'He was immortal except for his heel. It was his one weak spot, so that's where Paris shot the arrow that killed him.'

'Right!' I said.

'What does that have to do with us winning, though?' asked Allie.

'The Shiners are seven puffed-up egos,' I said. 'They all think they're going to stroll through the second half and score one more goal. Did you see how they sauntered off at half-time? Even if we get another goal in the second half, they'll make sure they get a couple more just to obliterate us. They're full of themselves. The thing is, they've forgotten that every team has its strengths. They don't play like a team – not like we do,' I said.

'Yes, that's our strength,' said Talia. 'We need to play like the team we are and catch them off guard when they think it's safe,' she said slowly.

Seven puffed-up egos would never stop to think that we could act as a proper team. A team with a plan.

I gestured to everyone to lean in, and looked around to make sure Beehive wasn't lurking nearby. She wasn't. I could see the other players and Mrs Chatton all the way over on the other side of the pitch, looking pretty pleased with themselves. The Shiners and their supporters were certain it was over for us. My stomach fluttered a little. What if they were right? What if our dream was over? But then Mãe's words came to mind: *Shoot for the stars!* Yes, I would! I was going to play the best game ever and do what I could to lead my team to victory.

I closed my eyes and ordered my thoughts before I started again. 'So, this is what we need to do . . .'

Five minutes later, we had agreed on our plan of action.

'What if it doesn't work?' Talia frowned.

'But what if it does?' I said.

The Bramrock Stars filed back out, an army trooping off to our starting positions, ready to put our plan into action and win this final battle. The whistle went for the second half to start and we moved across the pitch with short, sharp passes.

As we predicted, the Shiners didn't waste any time in pulling ahead with another goal. Then they had a long and showy celebration. It was obvious they thought they had it in the bag. After that, they just wanted to play it safe, with all their forwards crowding round to support the defence.

'Two minutes,' Rhiannon called out.

It was time for action.

Dribbling the ball down the right wing, I paused and did a dummy kick with my right leg, crossing it to Talia with my left. She looked unsure as she stopped and brought the ball under control. She wavered for a split second, looking from me to the goal. I knew what she was thinking. I shook my head and pointed both my index fingers at her. *Stick to the plan, Talia!*

I positioned myself in the best spot. Immediately, the Shiners' goalie edged towards me while all their defenders encircled me like bees to a honeypot. *Perfeito!* Our plan was working perfectly. I watched as Talia scooped the ball up and over in a perfect arc. It sailed past the bewildered defenders, curving slowly and gracefully towards the goal, towards its target. Suddenly, everything seemed to be in slow motion.

It was a race between the ball and the goalie.

Can we really do this? I hardly dared to look.

The Shiners' goalkeeper leaped across the goal, her face scrunched up in desperation as she stretched out her arms . . .

35

Um, Dois, Três

GOAL!

Just as we'd planned, Talia's last-second goal had made sure we'd ended on two–all. That meant the game would be decided on penalties. *Ugh.* My plan had seemed like a good one at the time, but now I wasn't so sure.

The fast beats of my heart were loud thuds in my chest, my thoughts whirred round my head, and a nervous tremor ran up my right hamstring. The referee jogged over to us. 'Each team will have three shots at the goal. It's the best of three or, if both teams score the same, it goes to sudden death.'

We'd decided before that Talia, Steph and Layla were the best at taking penalties, but now Steph was out with her injured ankle. There was nothing else for it. I was going to have to take Steph's place, since Charligh and Naomie, as defenders, hadn't had as much practice at shooting at goal, so as captain I knew I had to step up ... *And anyway*, I kept thinking, *I'd rather shoot and fail than not try at all.*

Behind the goal I could see our teachers and parents and everyone from Bramrock Primary. Olly, Theo and the K triplets were leading a noisy chant they'd made up: 'Bramrock Stars ... don't hit the bar ... Bramrock Stars, BRING IT HOME!' Despite their loud cheers, they were still almost being drowned out by the orchestra of drums, horns and whistles of the Shiners' supporters. The chants and cheers of our side had far more heart.

This time, an equalizer wouldn't be enough, just like our supporters said – we had to bring it home. The only way to make sure we did was to get each of our three shots squarely in the goal.

We had three chances, just like the three wishes granted by a fairy godmother.

'After each penalty attempt,' the referee continued, 'the ball will go back to the position ready for the next attempt. You'll take it in turns: a player from one team, followed by a player from the other; for example, first Silvertown Shiners, then Bramrock Stars, then Shiners again, and so on.' She tossed a coin. It was heads to the Shiners, who chose to go first.

The crowd shushed themselves into silence. My palms were sweaty and clammy, but I gave a thumbs up to Allie in goal. For the first time ever, she was looking quite flustered.

Not now – please don't lose it now, I thought.

Number 2 from the Shiners ran up and swung her leg smoothly. The ball sailed up in a perfect arc and into the net.

First up for our team was Talia. She stood there without flinching, focused, ready to move and hit the ball. Again, silence fell on the pitch and in the crowd. As Talia ran up to the ball, one of the Shiners sneezed loudly. I glared at her, but as I turned back to watch the ball's journey, it was clear the attempt to distract Talia had failed. One–all!

Next, Jilly swaggered up. She stuttered as she kicked, which tricked Allie, who lurched to the left. But Jilly's manoeuvre had flicked the ball neatly up to the right. She was already turning round to cheer with the Shiners' fans before the ball had hit the back of the net.

Then it was Layla's turn. Her skin had a queasy sheen to it and she looked as if she wanted to be anywhere but inside the penalty box. She ran rather jerkily at the ball and her leg gave a flailing kick. The ball sailed to the right and the goalie lazily tipped it away from the crossbar, but it bounced off a rogue bump in the ground and rolled into the net. I let my breath out. That was close. Two–all!

Our fans went wild and the chanting got even louder. 'Watch out, watch out, we're here, we're here, WE'RE HERE! Let's shout, let's cheer! Let's shout, let's CHEER FOR THE STARS!'

There was quiet again after that. Victoria Chatton was up next for the Shiners. She walked up stiffly to the ball and Allie crouched forward, her legs planted wide. I felt a twinge of pity for Victoria. I'd be nervous with a mum like hers watching me. She kicked out and the ball spun low and wide. I watched its journey. Too wide!

Allie swooped low and the ball hit her cupped gloved hands with a wonderful thud. A save! Still two– all – and we still had our last shot to go!

This was it. My turn. My mouth was drier than sawdust and I wiped my clammy palms on the side of my shorts.

'Come on, Jaz! We're counting on you,' I heard Theo shout from the sides.

My stomach twisted.

Thanks for that, Theo, I thought. I knew he didn't meant to make me more nervous, but I could have done without the added pressure just then. *Life isn't Jenga*, Mãe had said. Everything won't all come crashing down on me, no matter what happens next. I took a deep breath.

Then I faced the goalkeeper and tilted my head up, trying to look braver than I felt to keep the nerves down. *Focus!*

But suddenly there was a confusing crowd of voices in my head: *miscreant . . . minha anjinha . . . loser, you never learn, do you? . . . star striker . . . failure . . . you can do this . . . can't . . .*

I shook my head, trying to clear my mind. *Focus! . . . Heaps of love. A cup of hope . . . A spoonful of courage.*

I ran towards the ball and swung my left leg. For a split second it felt like someone had pressed the pause button on the world and everything else had stopped. But I was still moving. I kept my eyes straight ahead of me as my foot connected with the ball.

It sailed away from me and rolled over the line, like a marathon runner reaching her destination, then it came to a tired stop in the safety of the net.

It took me a moment to understand properly. I'd scored a penalty. I'd scored our goal number three.

Suddenly, the referee was blowing her whistle and the final score was three–two to us. The trophy was coming home!

My eyes went a bit bleary, so I squeezed them shut. *Please don't let this be another one of my dreams!* I opened them again – and everything was clear. A resounding cheer had gone up from our small crowd of supporters. I could see purple stars, but they weren't the ones on my ceiling. The stars were right here with me on the pitch. A deafening cheer went up from our supporter corners. They were cheering because . . .

we . . .

. . . did

. . . it!

The Stars were jumping, whooping and hugging each other, and our supporters had spilled out on to the pitch to join us.

The Shiners looked on gloomily. I almost felt sorry for them. I led my team as we filed past the losing team, shaking the hands of the Shiners' players and congratulating them on a great game. That was something we could all agree on – it was a match to remember.

'Well done,' said an unsmiling Jilly as she shook my hand. 'You got it this time, but we'll be back.'

'Thanks! See you next time,' I said.

And no doubt the Shiners would be back, but so would we.

*

After Dad had congratulated me with the biggest bear hug imaginable, Rhiannon introduced me to Gayle Gallagher, the senior sports reporter on the *Brighton Chronicle*. Gayle was armed with a tiny voice recorder that doubled up as a pen, and a notepad where she had already made some scribbles. A camera swung from her neck. She pointed the recorder at me, so it was just a few inches from my mouth.

'So, Jasmina – team captain! How does it feel to be the first team in Bramrock Primary to bring home a regional cup in over fifteen years?'

First I did a bit of a goldfish impression, opening and closing my mouth a few times. Then I choked out a few words about being *um, very, really, super happy*. Finally, I was saved by Charligh who was definitely made for the media.

'It feels wonderful!' she gushed in her very best I-was-born-to-be-famous voice. 'Like we always say – the Stars are dreamers who never gave up.' I wondered how long she'd been practising that speech.

The other Stars gathered round and everyone wanted to chip in and have their say. After Gayle hit the stop button on her voice recorder, she took a team picture and told us she already had lots of action shots of us running, dribbling and shooting during the game. The article would be published in next week's *Brighton Chronicle*.

'Any final words from the team captain?' Gayle said as the crowd around us began to disperse.

I nodded, finding my voice again as I thought of what Charligh had said: *The Stars are dreamers who never gave up*. She was right, and together we had shone brightest when we worked as a team.

'Well, I never thought I'd say this,' I said, 'but I guess you could call us the dream team!'

36

A Toast!

The next hour passed in a dizzy swirl of happiness. First there was the awards presentation. A small stage had been set up for this and the mayor spoke a few words about how all the teams had displayed hard work, discipline and dedication to reach this stage.

'And now for the important bit,' said the mayor, 'the presentations! I'd like to welcome to the stage Alana Young, a former player for Brighton and Hove Albion WFC and former coach of the national women's team.' A smartly dressed woman in a blue-and-white suit stepped up to the microphone.

My eyes widened. 'Wow! A Seagull is presenting our medals,' I gasped.

'I don't much like the sound of that,' Allie said. 'What if it flies away before giving them to us?'

'No,' whispered Naomie. 'The Seagulls is the nickname for the team. Like the England team are called the Lionesses.'

'What's our nickname, then?' Allie said.

I hadn't thought of one before but now I had the perfect name. 'Dreamers!'

Allie grinned. 'I like that!'

Before Alana handed out the medals, she talked about how much the game had moved on in the past decade and how women footballers were becoming more well known. 'But, despite women's football being the fastest-growing sport in Britain, there are a lot of issues that still need to be addressed,' she said. 'There's still inequality in the coverage we get in the media. And there's the gender pay gap too – women footballers don't earn as much as their male counterparts.

'It's clear that there's a system in place that marginalizes women's football. And we see evidence of this in operation from the school and junior stage, right up to professional adult levels. Many people think we aren't as serious, committed or talented as male players, but let me tell you: they're wrong! Aren't they, girls?'

We all cheered and nodded, and I felt proud to think we were all playing our part in changing that story by showing that girls could *definitely* be as committed to playing the beautiful game! Maybe one day it would be me standing there, handing out medals to young girl footballers.

And, who knows, perhaps things would be fairer and more equal by then, so we wouldn't have to spend our time talking about sexism at our awards presentations.

After she'd finished her speech, we all went up one by one on the stage to get our medals and shake Alana's hand. When we were all squeezed on to the stage, Alana turned to a little table at the side and picked up the trophy. It was a beauty: burnished bronze and on the bottom a gleaming golden plaque where the dates and team names would be engraved. Ours would be the very first to be inscribed.

'So finally,' said Alana into the microphone, 'please give a huge round of applause to the Bramrock Stars, the first winners of the Brighton Girls' Under-elevens Seven-a-Side Football Tournament. I'd like to ask Jasmina Santos-Campbell, their captain, to step forward and receive the trophy. Well done, girls!' And, still feeling as if I was in a dream, I walked towards Alana and she handed me the trophy.

I could see Dad looking as pleased as punch when I lifted it up, but I didn't remember much after that except giving a huge goofy grin as Gayle took one more picture of us all with the trophy and our medals.

Finally, there was a celebration party in the indoor sports hall for all the teams and their supporters. There were three long tables filled with fruit, sandwiches, crisps and juice.

Dad and Rhiannon came over with Alana.

'Hi, Jaz,' Rhiannon said with a grin. 'I thought you might like to have a chat with Alana.'

I nearly choked on my grapes. Here I was talking to THE Alana Young. She shook my hand again and congratulated me on an amazing game – and especially my winning penalty kick!

Then she invited me and the Bramrock Stars to a training session she was running with the Seagulls after the Christmas holidays.

'That would be amazing! Thank you so much,' I gasped.

'No, thank *you*,' Alana said. 'I think you could teach us a lot with that lethal left foot you showed taking that penalty, not to mention your magical dribbling skills!'

'Did that just really happen?' I asked as Alana strolled off to chat with some other people.

Rhiannon smiled. 'By the way, I've rung Steph's mum. The X-ray showed her ankle wasn't broken, thank goodness. It's just a very nasty sprain. She'll have to wear an ankle support over the next few weeks, but she should be back at our training sessions in the New Year.'

I sped over to the rest of the Bramrock Stars, who were gathered round one of the tables, and shared the good news about Steph and the invitation to train with the Seagulls.

'Let's do a toast,' Charligh said, holding up a glass of apple juice.

'To what?' Allie asked, swallowing hard on her mouthful of crisps.

Everyone grabbed a glass and held it high. Naomie held up two – 'One of them's for Steph,' she explained.

'To friendship, and family . . .' Layla said.

'To football,' said Talia.

'To us,' I said.

'To Dreamers,' we said in unison, and our glasses met with a happy clink.

37

A Slice of Love

'*Parabéns!* Congratulations – again!' Aunty Bella said, kissing me goodbye.

Finally, it was time to go home.

Mrs Gorley took Charligh, Naomie and Talia home, while Allie and Layla went with Mrs Hussani. I hurried over to Rhiannon, who was heading off to meet some friends.

'Thanks for everything, Rhiannon.'

'I should be thanking *you*,' Rhiannon said. 'Moving away from my family to a new city and starting college has been exciting for me, but it's been difficult not having any real friends till now. Coaching Bramrock Stars FC has given me the confidence I needed to go out and meet new people.'

'You've got thousands of friends, though!' I said incredulously.

'Not in real life. Social-media followers aren't the same as real friends,' Rhiannon said.

It's funny – I'd always thought adults, even young ones like Rhiannon, had everything all sorted out in their heads. But I could see they still felt scared, had doubts and got their feelings muddled up, just like us kids. No one had everything figured out completely, and that was OK. Everyone was still learning all the time. Learning wasn't just something you did at school.

Rhiannon went on: 'Talking about real friends, Jaz, I wish I'd been part of a team like yours when I was growing up. You really look out for each other, on and off the pitch.'

I smiled after she walked off. She was right. Football might have brought us together, but friendship had *kept* us together. Some of us had never spoken to each other before we formed the team. There was Layla, who cried over practically everything, whether she was happy or sad; Talia, who loved memorizing rules; Naomie, who could be relied on to explain the laws of physics to us; Charligh, who treated the pitch as her very own theatre stage; Allie, who had struggled to keep her hands still and her temper cool; and Steph, who worried about everyone. Oh, and of course me, the one who nearly let my fears get the better of me and almost threw it all away. And yet, when things had got really stormy, we'd done what stars do: we'd shone even brighter in the darkness.

I fastened my seat belt as Dad drove slowly through the car park towards the exit. Everything had been so exhausting, not just the game, but facing my fears and being truthful with everyone over the past week too.

'I called and told your mum the good news while you were all celebrating,' Dad said. 'I even videoed the penalty shoot-out and sent it to her.'

'Thanks, Dad!' I squealed. I was thrilled Mãe had seen the final minutes, even if it was on video. I pulled out my phone. No message from her, though. 'I hope Mãe's design event went well,' I said. 'My dream has come true today and I hope hers has too.'

'Yes, me too,' Dad said quietly.

'I don't want you both to be angry at each other any more . . . and I love you and Mãe both the same –' My words tumbled out in a hurry.

Dad looked astonished. 'Of course, love. You never have to pick sides, Jaz. We're a whole team: me, you, your mum and Jordan. Even if we do score some own goals sometimes.'

I stole a glance up at Dad. 'When Mãe left us . . . you seemed angry at her. I didn't know if I should have been angry too.'

Dad switched the indicator on: *tick-tock, tick-tock*. He turned into a side street, drew up at the kerb and took the key out of the ignition. The purr of the engine died down to nothing. Finally, he spoke.

'Sometimes I don't always react to things the way I should, and it's so easy for hurt to turn into anger. But I've never stopped thinking the world of her – and you mustn't stop either. I don't know if we can work it out, but – no matter what – you can always be sure of our love for you and Jordan.' Dad paused. 'I . . . I sometimes wonder . . . Perhaps *I* should have moved out like we'd planned . . .'

My eyes widened. 'Wait . . . what? *You* were going to move out, Dad? And Mãe wanted to stay?'

He nodded. 'Your mum and I . . . we'd been talking about it, but after the fire she . . . we . . . decided it should be her. I don't think she could even trust herself after that. And I didn't exactly help her feel great about it. I can see that now.'

I'd spent so much time worrying about what I thought were the worst situations in my head, but what had really happened wasn't anything like I'd imagined.

Back home, when I walked up the front path, I saw Jordan's face pop out from behind the curtain, then disappear again. I stepped inside, and gasped: a huge banner stretched the length of the stairs. It said, in Jordan's handwriting: 'Congratulations, Jaz!'

My brother stood at the bottom of the stairs, grinning.

Then Mãe appeared. Her puffy fringe had a dusting of flour on it and she was wearing a long saffron-yellow dress made out of some of her colourful wax-print fabric. It looked like sunshine against her deep-brown skin and the whole house seemed to light up. She was holding a magnificently lumpy cake. Most of the white icing was piled up on one side, like snow at the side of a path after it's been dug clear. Over the white frosting, written in sprawling lilac icing, was the message:

Parabéns!
To our Jaz –
Always Shoot for the Stars!

Noticing Dad's amused expression as he eyed the lopsided cake, Mãe laughed. A wonderful, contagious laugh that spread to me, then Jordan, and circled back round again to Dad like a golden boomerang. Mãe shook with laughter and the cake wobbled. Dad grabbed it, just in time to stop a cake avalanche. They placed it on the table and then Mãe cut a slice.

'The first slice is for you, princess,' Dad said.

Mãe had never made a cake in my whole life before, and this one was pretty funny-looking. I took a cautious bite.

'It's rotten, isn't it?' she groaned.

The light, airy sponge and creamy icing melted in my mouth. It tasted of vanilla, of cinnamon, of sweetness and love.

'No, it's *perfeito*. Thank you. *Obrigada!*'

38

The Beginning . . .

Brighton was so pretty at night – all the Christmas lights were up so the city was shimmering, and twinkling and gleaming under the velvet black sky. We walked right down North Street, then through the winding, twisting cobbled streets of the Lanes, then back round to the Boardwalk, which was buzzing with roller skaters, smoochy couples, loud families and curious tourists.

Despite all the lights and noise of Brighton at night, something about the salty sea air and the gentle swoosh of the waves me made me feel quite peaceful.

'I think that's enough walking,' Mãe said. 'We're going to turn into icicles out here.' My teeth chattered in agreement.

A few minutes later, we were warming ourselves in Mr Henry's, an American-style diner famous with locals and tourists for its delicious and juicy burgers, unusual-flavoured milkshakes, and fresh seafood. Mãe and I were in a booth, sitting on soft red-leather seats at a black table. A jukebox in the corner blared out a mixture of old and new hits. We'd both ordered our usual – the Spicy Bean Burger for me, and a seafood mixed grill for Mãe.

When the friendly waiter brought our food (with a cheerful, 'Enjoy!', which sounded as though he meant it), I sank my teeth into the bean burger. *Mmm!* It tasted even better than the last time.

'Your dad and I used to come here all the time and get the all-day breakfast,' Mãe was saying. 'We used to treat it as our mobile office as we got to grips with accounts and taxes and all the other stuff that goes with running a business. Dad used to have his own artisan design business before we had Jordan. That's when he started working for the council – the hours were better for fitting round childcare.'

It was surprising to hear my mum talk about times in the past that included Dad. It was nice.

'The last time I came here with him, though, everything had changed so much,' she continued.

I peered at the menu. 'Are you sure?' I said. I'd been coming here since I was about five years old and I couldn't remember the menu changing once.

She laughed. 'No, not the menu. That's probably older than you. So is the jukebox in the corner – and these old leather seats. Your dad had changed. He was into all that healthy stuff, so he stopped ordering the steak roll like before. The last time we came he ordered a bean burger, like you're eating right now, actually.' She smiled, but she looked a bit defeated. 'Maybe I haven't changed enough.'

There was a short silence. Mãe played with her napkin, and I decided to tell her how I felt.

'I know you think you're not as good as Dad at looking after us,' I began. 'But I – we, Jordan and me – we need you too. I need both of you,' I said.

Mãe looked surprised but didn't say anything as she moved round so she was next to me on the seat. It gave me more courage to go on.

'One day you were there, and then the next you were gone. It's all been so different, but we've had to pretend as if nothing's changed. I wondered – are you disappointed you've got a daughter like me because I do everything all wrong?'

I said that last bit very quietly because I half hoped she wouldn't hear, but at the same time I needed her to. My worst fear had gnawed at me for so long. It had weighed me down like I was under a huge boulder, until I felt that all my hope was being crushed. Now I'd spoken it out loud and, no matter what the answer was, it felt so good to have got it off my chest. I felt lighter than I had done in months.

'Disappointed?' Mãe echoed, looking at me as if I'd just said there was a giraffe in the room. 'D'you think I always do the right thing, *anjinha*? I have two beautiful children and a wonderful husband and yet I'm living in my younger sister's spare room.'

'I wasn't sure you cared,' I said. 'Not just about moving out . . . but about everything to do with me. You never come to parents' evenings at school, and you didn't even stay to watch the whole game the first time you saw me play.'

'Shall I tell you why I stopped coming to parents' evenings, Jaz? I hated hearing your teachers saying you were always daydreaming, that you weren't dotting your i's and crossing your t's. Ms Morgan used to let you shine, though. That's why I used to love coming to the dance showcases. When you started the football team, I was so happy, because football's where your heart has always been. The only reason I left that game early was because your dad and I had had a row and I was so annoyed. I didn't want to stay and create a scene and upset you. Me and your dad, we need to start talking again, to sort things out, but that isn't your responsibility – it's ours. I'm *so* sorry for making you feel it was your fault. You're more than good enough, *princesa*. I'm so lucky to have the kindest, bravest, funniest daughter in the world. And, if anything, you've inspired me.' Her dark brown eyes glittered with tears.

I was gobsmacked. I'd obviously totally misunderstood her actions all this time. 'I "inspired you"?' I repeated.

Mãe smiled. 'Seeing your determination to build that team gave me the push I'd needed to do something I'd been dreaming of for ages. I've wanted to build my own fashion label for years. So yesterday, while you were at the final, I went to that fashion event to present my designs at a special business-pitch session they were holding. And, well, they loved them – and my plans to sell across the country and beyond – so I got the funding!' She beamed as she pulled out a glossy business card with an African print design on the back and held it out to me.

'JJ's Designs,' I read aloud.

'It stands for Jaz and Jordan – my two diamonds, who inspire me to follow my dreams and always shoot for the stars too.'

I tingled all over with excitement. 'Congratulations, Mãe. Soon the whole world will see how talented you are.'

Mãe smiled, and this time her eyes did too. 'Talking of talent, I'm convinced you'll play for England one day. But do you know what makes me a million times happier even than seeing you scoring goals? You, Jaz. Just as you are. Win or lose. You're always a star.'

I thought for a moment, then said, 'Let's start again, Mãe. A new beginning?'

'Yes, I like the sound of that. New starts for the new stars,' she said, and she kissed the top of my head. 'Now, let's have that special dessert I promised you, shall we?'

We ordered a sharing dessert, our favourite – the Hot Brownie Fudge Mountain of Ice Cream Delight – and a short while later we were working through creamy ice cream layered with hot, chewy brownies and a mound of cream delicately balanced on top. We ate slowly, slurping it right down to the last trickle of delicious fudge-streaked cream. Then Mãe held me tight and this time I hugged her right back.

I thought about what my parents had said over the last week and what I had figured out for myself. I didn't know if Mãe was coming back to live with us at home on Half Moon Lane. She probably didn't know herself yet. But that was all right. They'd sort something out. And, wherever she was, I knew now that she would still be there for me somewhere, in her own way. It was like the stars, I thought. *We can't always see them but we know they're up there.* I also knew that when things didn't feel right, I could speak up, even if sometimes my voice shook. Even if sometimes my mind created monsters and fear, I could use my imagination to dream big dreams.

I looked out of the window at the dark purple sky speckled with jewels of light. The bright stars glittered and danced high above us as the colour gave way to the creeping darkness of the soft black night. It wasn't always easy to shoot for the stars, but it would always be worth it.

Epilogue

Between you and me, I wish I could tell you that Mãe and Dad never, ever argued again. I wish even more that I could tell you that Mãe moved back in, but for now she's still at Aunty Bella's. I also wish Ridiculous Rosie had stopped being so terribly annoying . . . but we don't always get everything we wish for. *On the other hand*, I thought as I looked at the Brighton Sevens medal I'd put round Kinsley's neck in place of the Reds scarf, *sometimes we do*.

Mãe comes round a lot more nowadays, and she and Dad are arguing a lot less. They even laugh together sometimes, especially when Mãe stays for dinner. Yesterday she took me for a day out in London, just me and her. We went on the London Eye and I took some great photos from the top.

One of the first things I did when we went back to school after the tournament was to thank Zach on behalf of all the Bramrock Stars. He muttered something terribly rude – far too rude for me to repeat, I'm afraid – before stomping off. He thought I was winding him up, but I was truly grateful to him, and to the VIPs too. If it hadn't been for them, maybe I wouldn't have started Bramrock Stars FC!

Mr Roundtree offered to coach us for the rest of the season. He said I could do with his pearls of football wisdom if I wanted to play professionally one day. I told him he could keep them – we were sticking with Rhiannon, and she was chuffed to bits.

In other news the *Brighton Chronicle* mentioned the dance showcase in a tiny article with small print that you could just about see if you used a magnifying glass. Rosie was fuming because her mum had sent the *Chronicle* professional photos of Rosie in her sapphire-blue dress, but the paper didn't print any of them. And although I don't want to rub it in (of course not!) the *Chronicle* did a special two-page-spread spotlight feature on 'The Dream Team'. My name was in the paper: 'Jasmina "Jaz" Santos-Campbell, the enterprising founder and team captain of Bramrock Stars who went from pirouettes to penalties'! They even had a quote from Alana Young, who described me as a 'likely future England star' and 'the mesmerizing new talent who could be Bramrock's answer to Rachel Yankey'. Fancy that!

'Wonders never cease,' Mrs Forrest had murmured after Miss Williams displayed the article on the whiteboard and read out the best bits in assembly. I'm almost certain I saw a twinkle in Fussy Forrest's eye, though. Mind you, it could have been a glint.

'I know,' I'd said. Well, at least we'd finally agreed on something!

I'd love to stay and chat, but training is calling and I can't wait to get started . . . Sorry – what was that? You thought our story was ending? Oh no, this is just the beginning!

So *tchau* for now. (That's 'bye' in Portuguese, by the way.)

Love,

Jaz Santos-Campbell xxx

Left Striker and Team Captain, Bramrock Stars FC

☆ Q&A with author ☆
Priscilla Mante

What inspired you to write *Jaz Santos vs. the World*?

I think it was a combination of a few things! I've worked with children from a range of backgrounds, and I've seen young people banding together to seek change while also remaining hopeful in challenging situations. More generally, I've often witnessed people who wrongly think they're always to blame for the difficult experiences they've had. So I wanted to write a story that had a different take on that and also inspire hope, determination and the pursuit of dreams.

Why did you decide to focus on football in this series? What does football mean to you?

My goal was to write a story that was meaningful but also lots of fun! I love sport, and playing football was one of my favourite ways to spend my time when I was younger.

The beautiful game is a sport, but I also view it as an art: a way of expressing yourself, communicating and connecting with others. From professional league to street football and everything in between, I've seen football bridge barriers between cultures, create a sense of unity, and spark hope among communities and individuals.

Do you have a favourite character in the story?

I love all my characters – even the villains – so that's a tough one! I wouldn't say I have a favourite but I feel like I know Jaz the best because telling this story from her perspective took me on a journey with her. Writing is a process of discovery – I'm so excited about getting to know the other characters just as well when I write their stories!

What is your favourite scene in the book?

I think it's after the finals when Mãe surprises Jaz with the gloriously misshapen cake. Partly because I love cake, but also because it makes me smile to imagine Jaz, after what she's been through, having this joyous celebration with all her family. I hope it makes readers smile too.

Did you always know you wanted to be an author?

Yes, definitely – as a young child I became convinced of how incredibly wonderful and transformative books were. So, when I wasn't reading stories, I spent a lot of time making my own up and acting them out with my dolls. I also decided one of the best things I could do when I grew up was to become a writer of some sort. However, I was a bit worried that when I was older I'd forget about children's books and write only for adults. When I was around nine I made a solemn promise to my future self that, if I did make it as an author, my very first book would be for children! I feel very blessed to have been able to achieve that dream – I think younger me would be extremely happy that I did.

Do you have any advice for aspiring authors?

☆ Read, and read widely! There is no one way to write, but reading a variety of things like books, poetry, comics, playscripts and even articles will help you find your own writing style and learn more about crafting a compelling story.

☆ Practise writing your own stories. Characters are at the heart of every story, so work on creating memorable and realistic characters who can take the reader on a meaningful journey over the course of the story.

☆ Keep a journal – no matter how ordinary you think your life is. Consuming art forms such as books, films, theatre and TV productions is also super helpful for enhancing your creativity and imagination. However, there's so much inspiration to be gained from real life.

☆ And, lastly, don't give up!

What were your favourite books growing up?

I had so many but to name a few: *Anne of Green Gables*, *Matilda*, *Maizon at Blue Hill* and the Babysitters Club series.

Did any books or authors inspire you to write the Dream Team series?

The Babysitters Club series by Ann M. Martin – I really loved that it had a diverse cast of characters and how relatable each character was. My favourites were the two junior club members – Mallory and Jessi!

Also, I discovered Jacqueline Wilson's books as an adult because her writing was immensely popular with the young people I worked with. I think her stories are wonderful, and she manages to combine tackling difficult issues with believable characters and engaging plots.

What is the one thing you'd like readers to take away from this story?

You are more than the sum of your experiences, and your future doesn't need to be defined or limited by your past or present circumstances. Your dreams matter – I hope you shoot for the stars!

What will your next book be about?

The next book centres on Jaz's best friend, Charligh, as she takes the spotlight as the lead in the school play. It's about the celebration of difference and embracing your true self even when you don't fit in.

Jaz's Spiced Apple & Cinnamon Cake

Please follow this recipe with an adult supervising, and take care when using a hot oven.

Cake ingredients

200 g wholewheat plain flour

2 teaspoons baking powder

½ teaspoon bicarbonate of soda

140 g caster sugar

2 apples, peeled, cored and roughly chopped

2 eggs*

1 teaspoon vanilla essence

120 ml of vegetable oil

110 ml of yoghurt*

1 teaspoon ground cinnamon

½ teaspoon ground nutmeg

½ teaspoon ground cloves

1 apple, peeled, cored and finely sliced

Cinnamon crumb topping ingredients (optional)

50 g sugar

1 teaspoon cinnamon

1 tablespoon melted butter (or dairy-free alternative)

*Make it vegan:

- Replace eggs with 130 g unsweetened apple sauce or 2 small mashed bananas.
- Use dairy-free yoghurt.

1. Preheat the oven to 180°C (160°C if using a fan oven). Grease and line a round 23-cm (9-inch) cake tin with baking paper.

2. Sift the flour into a large mixing bowl, and add the baking powder, bicarbonate of soda, sugar, cinnamon, nutmeg and cloves. Add the chopped apple and mix briefly to combine.

3. In a separate bowl add the eggs (or your vegan alternative), vanilla essence, oil and yoghurt. Whisk briefly (this will break up the egg yolk, if using).

4. Add the wet ingredients to the dry ingredients, stirring lightly until it's all combined – but take care not to over-mix.

5. Pour the cake mix into the greased cake tin and arrange the apple slices on top in a circular pattern. Sprinkle with a little extra caster sugar and cinnamon if desired.

6. For the cinnamon topping: mix the sugar, cinnamon and melted butter together until the mixture forms a wet lumpy consistency. Evenly spoon the topping on top of the apple slices.

7. Bake in the centre of the oven for approximately 35–40 minutes, or until a skewer inserted in the middle comes out clean.

8. Transfer to a rack and leave to cool completely.

9. Serve with vanilla ice cream or cream if desired!

Jaz's Dream Team

3 — Jaz Santos

11 — Rachel Yankey

9 — Vivianne Miedema

6 — Megan Rapinoe

10 — Asisat Oshoala

8 — Marta

2 — Saki Kumagai

7 — Rachel Corsie

4 — Crystal Dunn

5 — Carole Costa

1 — Becky Spencer

Afterword

Jasmina Santos-Campbell is a mischievous, anxious and determined little girl with big dreams and great empathy. I started her story from a point where she's experiencing the uncertainty and tumult of fractured relationships in her family, but as I wrote I discovered there was so much more to tell about Jaz. The first draft of this book was centred on Jaz's response to her parents' separation, with football very much in the background. Over time, as I reflected on and revised my manuscript, Jaz's voice and character became stronger and clearer in my head and I knew there was another story to tell.

One about a girl passionate and ambitious about the beautiful game that she lived and breathed. She followed her dreams while battling the negative internal voices that told her she was inadequate, and fought to dismantle and challenge a system that made things harder for her. Most of us can relate to worrying about whether we are good enough, or the fearful reluctance to follow or even voice our dreams. And we can all see that, sadly, not everyone in our world is treated equally.

I grew up just outside Glasgow and I used to play football most days with my classmates. I'd usually be the only girl on the field, but I'm happy to say, unlike Jaz, I have happy memories of being welcomed on the pitch by most of the boys. When I was ten, the coach of my town's professional football team came to visit my school. He led a training session and let us show him our skills. I can still remember the surprise and pride I felt when he pointed me out, asked my name and urged me to join a girls' football team. For a moment I felt like maybe one day I could be a football star! I loved football, almost as much as I loved reading and writing stories, but I never pursued it beyond my early teenage years.

Fortunately for me, I got to achieve an even bigger childhood dream of mine – writing books for children. But I think of all the young people and even adults who are discouraged from aiming for something because the world around them says, directly and indirectly, that they will never make it. I want them to challenge the status quo, and ask themselves and society, 'Why not?'

I also didn't want to shy away from the fact that there are elements woven into the fabric of our society that can work against us and hinder the pursuit of our dreams. This means that some people need to work twice as hard to get to the same place as others, which is massively unfair. In Jaz's story, I named sexism as the root of some of the obstacles she faced. This was shown in the dismissive attitude from Rotten Roundtree, the indignation of the boys when Jaz outplayed them, and the initial reluctance of the school to give the girls equal funding.

Women's football is the fastest-growing sport in Britain; in America, it is equal to the men's game in terms of audience ratings, and after the

World Cup in 2019 many women footballers have become household names globally. However, as the character Alana Young told us in the final chapters, there's still inequality in terms of pay, media coverage and overall respect. But things are changing, one game at a time.

I hope Jaz inspires everyone to always shoot for the stars, but also to remember you are more than the sum of your wildest dreams and deepest failures. Would Jaz and her wonderful team-mates be just as brilliant without their championship win? I think they would!

Jaz learned that being a star isn't about not feeling afraid or always winning. It's about doing the right thing and giving it your best, even if the odds are against you; it's about remaining hopeful, even if you don't get exactly the result you want.

I didn't give Jaz a fairy-tale ending. Maybe Iris and Drew do get back together, maybe they don't. However, as long as the readers know that Jaz can thrive and sparkle regardless, I think I've got my message across.

Thank you so much for reading, and I hope you'll come back to hear more stories from the Dream Team.

I'd like to finish with the words of Harriet Tubman, the late great American activist and abolitionist:

'Every great dream begins with a dreamer.'

Acknowledgements

So many wonderful people have helped and encouraged me on this journey to publishing. Truth be told, if I were to list them all and the ways in which they did so that would be a book in itself, but I will limit myself to a mere fraction of the names in these acknowledgements.

Sallyanne Sweeney, my brilliant agent who has loved Jaz and the Dream Team from the moment she read an extract of my book and worked with me tirelessly on multiple drafts before this went out to publishers. Thank you for believing in my writing, and for your incredible support all throughout this process.

Sara Jafari, my amazing editor who championed and recruited great support for the Dream Team within Puffin. Thank you for the passion and enthusiasm you've shown for working on my stories. And for your ongoing editorial genius in helping to reshape and polish this manuscript while understanding my creative vision and preserving the heart of my story. Thanks also to Naomi Colthurst for your enthusiasm and support for the Dream Team in the early stages when we had that initial editorial meeting in the offices of Penguin Random House. I hope by the time *Jaz Santos vs. the World* reaches bookshelves all of us can meet up for that long awaited celebratory lunch!

Thank you also to Shreeta Shah for your invaluable work on the copy-edits, and to Michelle Nathan and Phoebe Williams for your hard work and support on publicity and marketing. To everyone at Puffin who has worked on the Dream Team for all your wonderful work and for giving my book the best title – I am so thankful!

Thanks to the Commonword Children's Diversity Writing Prize for shortlisting the first draft of what is now *Jaz Santos vs. the World*. It was a very different version to this book we hold now, but it was the first writing competition I ever entered as an adult and being shortlisted based on the opening chapters gave me the impetus to complete the whole manuscript.

I'm so grateful to everyone at Spread the Word for your great support over the years! Thanks especially to everyone involved in delivering the inaugural London Writers Awards (LWA), a scheme that helped to reignite and reorient my journey to publishing. I'm grateful also to my fellow LWA awardees who have continued to cheer me on since the end of the programme.

Stuart White for creating the wonderful Write-Mentor community where I've gained various great opportunities to learn both as a mentee and a mentor. Thank you to everyone I've met through WriteMentor who has supported my book – you all play a part in making it a warm, accessible and supportive writing community!

Thank you also to Society of Children's Book Writers and Illustrators for all your ongoing advice and help, and for being such an amazing resource for children's writers!

For all my writer friends, so happy to have connected with you all. A special mention to

Asha who's not only a writing critique partner, but a fantastic friend who told me not to give up on this story back in 2018 when I was so close to putting it away forever!

To all the brilliant young people I've encountered in my work, thank you for everything you've taught me and for your open-heartedness!

Thank you to Afuah for cheering me along every step of the way – your enthusiasm for my writing has meant so much. Michelle, my oldest friend, for being on this journey with me in so many ways and being quite possibly the first person to pre-order copies of my book! Nikki, your amazing encouragement and help with everything, especially over the past couple of years! Sade, for your wonderful support always, and sharing my joy at every writing milestone.

To every single of one of my family, friends, former colleagues, from all around the world, who have cheered me on at one point or other, it has meant the world to me. Thank you also just for being bright stars in my life! I daren't try and name you all but you know who you are.

And to you, dear readers, the dream of you one day reading these pages and connecting with one of the characters has helped keep me focused on this journey. Thank you so much for visiting my fictional world! Working with Puffin to finalize *Jaz Santos vs. the World* over this year, 2020 – a year when the world has faced the shadowy backdrop of a pandemic – has been nothing short of joyous! Whatever is going on in the world when you read this book, I truly hope that it sparks hope and light in you too.

I'm also grateful to every closed door, and every rough path that ended in a dead end because it redirected me and it has led me to where I am today. And to that end I say thank you to God. The God who breathes life into my dreams, and who has kept showing me his unfailing love in the most uncertain of days and continually reminds me that a fall is not a fail.

Last but not least my mum, the bibliophile who shared her love of books with me, opened up her bookshelves to me when my own books ran out in between my regular library visits, and collected and stored all those stories I wrote as a child and agreed with no lack of certainty when I said I'd be an author. I won't forget the trouble you took when I was seven to get my alien space story typed up to enter in that writing competition, and how in your (obviously unbiased) judgement it was a winning entry despite the fact the judges clearly didn't agree. However, winners, like stars, are just dreamers who never gave up.

Enter Charligh Stage Next

Good evening, ladies, gentlemen, and most importantly: cats. You are all very welcome to the Charligh Gorley Show. My name's Charligh, and it may not or may not be spelled Charli on my birth certificate, but I think you'll all agree that the 'gh' gives it a bit more pizzazz. And, darling, there is nothing a girl like me, who is born for the stage, loves more than pizzazz . . .

Aside from being football famous, I also got the star role in my school musical. I thought it would be a breeze . . . *spoiler alert* it isn't.

That's the thing with the most marvellous of journeys. You might find yourself on the scenic route to your destination, and on the way you discover things you weren't even looking for.

Beware: There are twists, turns, detours, dead ends, false starts and, best of all, grand beginnings.

Look out for Charligh's story
the second book in

The Dream Team series
COMING IN 2022